T0032161

MATE OF HER OWN

By the Author

Pack of Her Own

Mate of Her Own

Visit us at www.boldstrokesbooks.com

MATE OF HER OWN

by

Elena Abbott

2023

THIS TRADE PAPERBACK ORIGINAL IS PUBLISHED BY
BOLD STROKES BOOKS, INC.
P.O. BOX 249
VALLEY FALLS, NY 12185

FIRST EDITION: OCTOBER 2023

CREDITS
EDITOR: JENNY HARMON
PRODUCTION DESIGN: STACIA SEAMAN
COVER DESIGN BY TAMMY SEIDICK

Acknowledgments

First and always, to my beautiful wife, my Goddess, my love. Without you this wouldn't exist. Without you I wouldn't be here. Thank you for putting up with me and seeing me through the rough times. You know what I'm talking about.

I'd like to thank my amazing editor Jenny Harmon for dealing with me as we edited my initial work into something people might actually want to read. I swear she's a mind reader, always understanding what I meant even before I did, and fixing the pesky issues that come from me trying to write like it's epic fantasy from the mid-80s. RIP my flowery prose.

To Alisha, who is always my first reader and one of my closest friends. I know I don't talk enough, but me sending random Word files to you is my love language. And Stephanie, who was the one who got me writing again a few years back. Neither this book nor the previous one would exist if it wasn't for you two.

Lastly, to my readers. I couldn't do this without all of you. Thanks for taking a chance on a mildly crazy person such as myself as I regale you with stories off the top of my head. It might be a little chaotic, but that's half the fun, isn't it?

To everyone who was forced to fit in as a child. I see you, I was you. Everyone finds their family, sometimes we just need to look.

To my Goddess, who found me.

PROLOGUE

Heather

As I took a swig of my beer I knew I blended in with the other regulars in this dingy bar. We were all here to drown our demons. It was a pity that mine knew how to swim.

I downed the rest of it before waving to the bartender, pointing to the now empty bottle. Another beer appeared on the bar in front of me, my fourth in almost as many minutes. I was hoping that things would start to feel bubbly and floaty, but I wasn't there yet. Not that I was going to stop trying. This was the only way I could think of to shut it up. The feeling that there was something inside me, something that wanted to break free.

Nineteen years old and I was busy trying to drown my feelings in alcohol. Probably not the healthiest choice, but it's not like my family cared, especially my mother. She didn't believe me when I told her. No one believed me. But how could they when the best way I could describe it was that there was a beast inside of me that wanted out so badly it hurt. Physically, emotionally, the pain was all-encompassing, and I was desperate to see if the booze would help.

Well, that and something else I wanted to try.

I turned away from the bar and scanned the dingy pub. The few tables were occupied by people who kept their heads down and their hands on their drinks. A flimsy railing separated the seating from a single billiard table that had a dim light swaying to and fro above it.

A short, dark-haired woman leaned against the wall, a pool cue held loosely in her hands as her partner took their shot. Sharp green eyes caught my gaze and held it for a long moment before she smirked. I glanced away, downing the rest of my beer and demanding another one.

"Ought to go easy on these, miss," the bartender drawled as he handed me another bottle.

I tossed a twenty on the bar and glared at him. "Just keep them coming."

I looked back at the pool table. The green-eyed beauty was lining up her shot. Her body leaned over the table, elbows and hips thrusting into the air as the cue moved back and forth in her thin fingers. I imagined what those hands might feel like wandering up and down my body and shivered. I knew what I wanted—what I needed now.

Not that I knew how to get it.

Then suddenly she was beside me, leaning over the bar with crossed arms. The bartender was at the other end, having a boisterous discussion with other patrons, and she turned to look at me, catching me with those eyes again.

"Keep your hand at the level of your eyes, puppy," she said.

"Did you just quote *Phantom of the Opera* at me?"

She laughed. "Most people don't get the line. I'm impressed, mutt."

I took another long swig of my beer, trying for an air of being too cool to pay attention to her antics. "Are you intending to throw a noose around my neck?"

She snorted, pulling back a little so she stood next to me. "Not me, but there's plenty of other wolves around here that would happily take a young little thing like you."

I shook my head. "Wolves? What are you talking about?"

She started to laugh again, but it died in her throat and she looked confused. "Do you—" She cut herself off, sniffing the air around me in a weirdly erotic way. "No, no, I smell wolf. Don't try to tell me you're passing yourself off as human?"

"Passing myself off..." I muttered, finishing the fifth beer. I laughed, deciding to play along. "Yeah, yeah, I'm messing with you. I am, like, totally a wolf and stuff. I'm just playing."

Her eyes were hard and serious. "It's dangerous here for someone like you. Wolf territory is on the other side of town. This is the Pride's place. You should know that."

I shrugged. "Maybe I wanted something different for a change."

She raised an eyebrow. "You don't say?"

"Yeah," I said, putting all of my faux courage and strength into my tone. "I'm sick of all the"—*What did she call them?*—"puppies and mutts."

She laughed again and a warm feeling washed through me. I wanted to bottle it and pull it out whenever I was feeling sad. She reached out and touched my hand, and a spark leapt between us. I looked at her with new eyes as hers narrowed.

"Did you...what are you?" she demanded.

I shook my head, unsure of what had happened. I rolled with it. "Like I said, I want something different." I turned my hand over and started rubbing her knuckles with my thumb. "I need something that the other puppies can't give me."

Her eyes caught the light and reflected, like a cat's eyes in the dark, and it took everything in me not to pull away. This was my chance. I needed to know if this was finally going to make me whole. If it didn't, I had no idea what else I could do.

She shook her head. "Kid, you're playing with things you don't understand."

"That's never stopped me from playing the game."

She watched me for a long moment, then glared at the bartender, who seemed to be avoiding our side of the bar. "Come." The word was said like a command, and I was off the stool and moving as if I hadn't downed five bottles of beer in less than ten minutes.

I expected to head for the front door, but she led me into the back instead. Her pool opponent gave both of us an odd look but didn't stand in the way as we passed the table into a back hallway. She threw open a door to the right and pulled me inside.

The bathroom was just this side of disgusting with a cherry of indecent on top. I almost expected to see a damned camera up on the wall. She followed in behind me and locked the door, then kicked open the empty stalls.

"What are you—" The words stuck in my throat as she spun with a snarl, one hand around my neck and the other on my cheek. She pushed hard until my back hit the wall and I moaned loud and long.

"Shut up, puppy," she snarled. There was no way I wasn't about to do what she asked. Her fingers gripped my throat tighter, and the world started to spin as I groaned and thrust myself toward her. Begging for anything that she'd give me. I needed it. Wanted it. Whatever it was inside me was desperate for it all. To feel something.

With one hand she raised me until my feet dangled. She quested downward with her other hand, forgoing most of me before reaching down into my pants.

She touched me and my mind went blank, my body moving as if it had a mind of its own. I felt something deep within roiling and writhing and trying to break free. I tried to let it go, to release it, but nothing changed, nothing helped. I sobbed aloud, as that same trapped feeling was everything.

Same as everything else I'd tried.

Same as always.

"Please!" I cried out as her fingers moved deftly inside me. My eyes opened and saw her face, closed with focus and intensity. Her eyes had changed, slipping into a strange color I'd never seen before. The pupils were slitted, like a cat's, and the lights caused a reflection in her eyes, and I gasped.

Then I felt it. Something tickling up my arms, my legs. I thought maybe it was the beginnings of my orgasm—I'd only ever orgasmed by myself before. But this was something else, something completely different. The feeling came in waves, coming and going like it couldn't make up its mind, and heat crept up my face as something started prying my gums apart. I opened my mouth and screamed.

"Fuck!" my beautiful partner shouted, and suddenly I was falling back on my ass, leaning back against the wall as she reappeared across the bathroom. "What the fuck? You can't even control it during sex? What is wrong with you?"

I shook my head. "What are you talking about?" I whipped my hands up to my mouth to double-check that everything was a proper size. Had I only imagined it?

"Puppy, you need to get your damned head on straight!"

"I don't know what you're talking about! What about your eyes? They went all weird and shit."

She stared for a long moment before rubbing a hand over her face. "You've got to be fucking kidding me. Haven't you shifted before?"

"Shifted?"

She shook her head. "No. No. I'm not dealing with this

tonight." She unlocked the door and opened it, pausing for only a second. "Figure out what you are, wolf, and don't show your face here again."

With that she was gone. I let myself flop onto the floor, breath still coming out in pants as I stared after her. What the hell had just happened to me? Who was I and why did it feel like I was trapped inside of myself? No matter what the question, there was only one person I could think of who might have the answer.

My mom was going to have a lot of explaining to do.

Chapter One

Heather

"So yeah, four years ago, that's how I found out I was a werewolf," I said, as if it weren't a big deal. I took a sip of my rum and Coke as Wren and Natalie stared at me. "What?"

"That's one hell of a wakeup," Wren said after a moment. "And I thought I had it bad when I shifted in the *shared* bedroom of my group home."

I laughed at that. "Oh, I need to hear this story."

Natalie smiled sheepishly. "You both already know my story," she said.

We all shared a laugh at that. Last summer had been a hell of a roller-coaster ride. Natalie had almost ended up dead and Wren was forced to turn Nat into a shifter to save her life. It was a hard transition at first, but Wren had managed to draw Nat's wolf out of her, and the two were finally together in every way that mattered to them.

Tonight, we were sitting out behind Wren's cabin, several tables set up with drinks and food and a bartender behind a makeshift bar. The cool spring air didn't stop the people milling around drinking and laughing. Most of the town's supernatural population was there, along with the few humans who knew what we were. That was what Terabend was, a supernatural sanctuary where werewolves and vampires and other nonhumans and humans could live in peace together. We lived here with the blessing of Vadi, the oldest among us. They called themselves a Genius Loci, and outside of Wikipedia I wasn't certain what that was. And tonight we were all here to celebrate Wren and Natalie.

Natalie let out a long sigh and looked to Wren. "I can't believe we're really doing this."

Wren looked almost embarrassed. "It's what you wanted, right?"

"Of course!" she insisted. "But we're already mates, I didn't expect you to propose!"

The majority of the partygoers were of the supernatural persuasion, so everyone heard that last word and raised their glasses with a cheer. The blush that flared up Nat's cheeks was adorable enough I almost wanted to heave. I couldn't blame her. After surviving last year, she deserved to be happy with Wren. And I totally wasn't jealous at all.

I didn't have the time to be jealous. I was too busy trying to figure out what the deal was with my wolf. For the first time since I was born, the being inside me was free, and I'd tried to draw her forth and speak with her, but she was holding a grudge. Outside of a couple times when we were in dire straits—like saving my Alpha from her kidnapper—my wolf had been a silent partner, only coming out on the full moons and refusing to communicate with me.

I glanced up as someone new joined our table. Danaan Rias, the witch who had helped break my curse last year, took a sip of something out of a martini glass and gave us all a smirk.

"Nat, your friend from the city is here."

"The cat?" Wren asked.

Natalie smacked her mate in the shoulder, and I laughed. "Be nice. She helped save you last summer." She got up with her empty glass and left with Rias, still chuckling.

"You're not a cat person, are you?" I said with a smile.

"What, do you think they'll take away my lesbian card for that?"

"Not a chance. Dogs count too, and Nat is as close to a pet as you're going to get for the time being."

My Alpha's face went a brilliant red and I chuckled, taking another sip of ineffectual alcohol. If it wasn't for the taste...

"Still can't believe you and Nat are tying the knot," I commented.

"It was important to her," Wren said, "and if I can do anything to make her understand that I'm not going anywhere, then I'm going to do it."

"What do you mean?"

Wren shook her head. "I don't blame her. She's got some abandonment issues. Asking her to marry me was the least I could do to help with that."

I jumped a little when I felt my phone vibrate in my pocket. I ignored it. The only people I wanted to talk to were here tonight. I had no idea who else would be calling.

"I hate to say it, but is this a good idea?"

"What do you mean?" Wren asked.

"After last year, with Jason and Craig, can we afford to draw attention to ourselves? Craig is still out there somewhere."

"We took care of it before, we can do it again, the three of us."

"Last time Natalie almost died, and we had half the supernaturals in Terabend helping us out. That might not be an option this time."

Wren put her beer down with a hard clunk. "Is there a reason you're bringing this up now?"

"I'm getting worried. It's been too quiet, and we don't have a pack to defend your territory."

"I don't want a pack like that."

"I know you don't," I said, "and I get it, I really do. But there's more to it than that. A pack is necessary for defending territory—or do you plan on taking care of it all yourself?"

"I don't know what I'm doing," she admitted. "All I know is that I don't want to start doing something like building an army for a threat that may or may not exist. I don't want that kind of pack, and you know that."

My phone started vibrating again. Wren gave me a look, her eyes flashing downward for only a second, and I shook my head. I didn't want to change the topic in the middle of this.

"I know. I understand that. There's plenty of wolves who wouldn't want to live the way we do. They wouldn't understand that we don't follow the traditional roles."

"It's a fucked-up system, is what it is. Everyone relying on an Alpha alone to make their lives better." Wren sighed. "You were in the Cardinals, you know what it was like. The bullshit about forcing mate bonds between the dominant and submissives to keep them in line. Holding pack bonds over the dominants' heads so they'll play nice and stay with the pack."

"You do know why, don't you?" I asked.

"What do you mean *why*? Because that's the way things have always been."

"Shit, you really didn't learn anything from your time with a pack, did you?"

Wren growled. "Be careful how you speak to your Alpha."

Last year I would have been quick to lower my head and take a submissive posture—something learned after years in another pack. But after spending so much time with Wren, I knew when to hold my head high. At least when it came to my Alpha, I knew where I stood.

"You know I'm not speaking against you. I'm just surprised you never heard the story."

"What story?"

"The story of when the shifters were almost completely wiped out centuries ago. I don't know the details, but it affected the way packs work since then. Every pack is desperate to keep the people they have, to remain strong, because the weaker the pack, the more likely they are to be destroyed."

"And they have to do it by forcing people to mate with others? By playing favorites? By treating those considered to be submissive like dirt? You know what I'm talking about. You looked like shit when you showed up last summer."

I cringed. "I am aware of the way the Cardinals treated me. I was considered the lowest of the low, barely above what they thought of humans. A wolf who can't shift? I was nothing but a liability."

Wren reached out and took my hand, holding it tightly. "No, you are certainly not a liability. And the wolves in our old pack were only used to looking at the surface, judging people by what they looked like and not for who they really are. They couldn't see beyond this stupid culture of dominants and submissives." Wren cracked a wide grin. "The only place people should be called dominant and submissive is in the bedroom."

I punched her in the shoulder. "Too much information, Alpha."

She laughed. "But you know that we will never be a pack like that."

"I know. And you think that if we bring in the wrong people, it will end up like that?"

She shook her head vigorously. "Who's to say? The wrong person could end up screwing up any good thing we have."

"So we won't look for anyone? Won't let anyone in? How is that a good idea?"

"I didn't say *that*," she snapped, "I just…We need to be careful."

I chose not to further aggravate the Alpha and backed off. We were both right. Last summer, Craig Reid from our old pack had kidnapped Wren with the intent of taking her for his mate and stealing her territory. Natalie, Wren's true mate, had been almost killed. She was only saved by Wren turning her into a werewolf. The upside was that Natalie survived and we stopped the encroaching wolves. The downside was that Craig survived and fled.

Wren was sure we wouldn't see him again, but I wasn't convinced. The man was all but feral back when I knew him. *Kidnapping an Alpha and killing her mate?* That he would think of trying it was unbelievable.

But she had enough to deal with right now. Teaching two new shifters how to communicate with their wolves and control their shifting was taxing on my Alpha. I could see it. Natalie was doing pretty good, becoming closer and closer with her wolf every time. It was hard to watch, when my wolf had all but cut off communication with me. I couldn't feel her the way the others could, or talk to her, or know what she was thinking. I couldn't remember the times I shifted outside of weird dreamlike snapshots that disappeared soon after shifting back again. And then there were the dreams—nightmares, really. Not always, but often enough that it felt like my wolf was getting back at me for something I couldn't even control.

After years locked away, it was like my wolf wanted

nothing to do with me, and both Wren and I were at a loss about how to fix it.

My phone started vibrating again and I pulled it out of my pocket, glancing at the caller ID. A number I didn't recognize. I hoped it was nothing.

"I should take this."

"It does seem insistent," Wren commented, as I stood up and moved away from the crowd.

I hurried to find a space where I could keep the conversation as private as possible. I couldn't say why, but there was a pit in my stomach as I answered the call.

"Hello?"

"Heather?"

I froze. "S-Summer?" I hadn't heard my sister's voice in years.

"Heather. You need to come home."

My low laugh was devoid of mirth. "I'm not welcome at home. You know that."

"This isn't the time to be petty," she said. "It's Mom. She's in the hospital."

"What?"

"It's Mom. She's sick. You need to come."

I stared across the yard at Wren, who was watching me with worried eyes. I took a deep breath. "Okay. I'll come home."

CHAPTER TWO

V

Tonight's job was easy, but not one I was looking forward to. I didn't understand why they had chosen a place like this for a gathering of this type. Why run the risk of involving humans in these things by setting them up in the middle of the damned city? There were plenty of wild spaces around here that would have kept us wolves hidden with only the light of the almost-full moon above to stand witness to what happened.

Instead, I was forced to find the security room of this multilevel car park and incapacitate the guard, then figure out on the fly how to disable the cameras to ensure our secrets. All while half the damned pack treated this like a tailgate party. I could hear their hooting and hollering from the damned security room.

With the cameras down, the hard drive pulled, and hopefully no sort of wireless backups, I left the security guard sleeping the sleep of the unconscious. I took my time finding the stairs and wandered up toward the fifth floor. It wasn't the top of the structure, but it wasn't near the bottom either. Hopefully we'd be done and out of here before anyone could complain of wild animals potentially mauling their vehicles.

Not that we'd have to worry about that if we'd picked a better place to do this shit.

But the thought of the spectacle was too great for the Alpha. A circle of wolves in human form, cheering and yelling and celebrating as two wolves went at it in the middle of the cold concrete. All watched over by the stern eyes of the Alpha.

It was barbaric. It was the way our culture worked.

I joined the rest of the wolves a few minutes later. As suited my position, I stepped up beside the Alpha and his Lupa. Or as I liked to call them, Mom and Dad.

"You're late," my dad, Desmond Raines, muttered out of the corner of his mouth. He towered over me by more than a foot, with shaggy black hair that fell to his shoulders almost like a lion's mane. When I was young I used to take solace in his strength, his imposing figure. Now I knew that it was truly one of his only weapons, a mask that he used to ensure people would not question him.

He kept his icy eyes on the crowd in front of us as two people stood on either side of the makeshift fighting circle. One of them was glad-handing the crowd, laughing and joking with those closest to him. His potential opponent, however, looked like he was going to be sick as he stared across the circle at the older man.

I shook my head. The poor kid looked like he was barely old enough to be in full control of his wolf. He shouldn't be here fighting tonight. Especially not against George Sinclair, the Enforcer for our pack, and not a man to challenge idly.

"Do you want your precious fights to be caught on camera for all the world to see?" I snapped back at the Alpha. My tone was borderline disrespectful.

"That's your job to handle," he said. "You're the one who wanted to be my Knight. Begged for the position, in fact."

I snorted. "Yeah, because I thought you might loosen the damned collar you've got around my neck."

"Darlings. This is not the time for your family squabble," my mother, Terra, said.

I bit back my retort and glanced over at her. My father earned my ire—often. My mother not so much.

I was told often that I looked more like her than my father, and I agreed. We had the same facial structure, similar height, and hazel-brown eyes. Only my hair took after my father, where my mother's hair was a lighter, almost blond color.

"Is the job done?" my father asked, as if we hadn't been about to get into an argument.

"Yes."

"Thank you, Knight."

Once more I bit my lip. My title was hard-fought and won, both verbally and in pit fights like the one that was getting ready to start. As the Knight, I was something of a troubleshooter for the pack, taking care of problems that arose, quietly and without fanfare. The job was different than that of the Enforcer, who was the head of the pack's fighting force that defended against other packs. My father had thought he could control my life, and fighting to become the Knight had been an attempt to break away. But somehow the position only served to draw me further into his orbit.

He liked to say we had the most progressive pack in western Canada. I said he was full of shit. Sure, there was a while there that he seemed to try to pull away from the decrepit culture that the wolf shifters followed, but it didn't last long. Of course, finding out your only child wasn't the daughter you wanted them to be could do that. But I knew who I was, and I wasn't about to let him dictate my life—that much. He still treated it like a phase, though I was twenty-eight and definitely not over it.

My thoughts were interrupted as my father moved forward, the crowd parting before him. He stopped at the edge of the circle, and both fighters, as well as the rest of the wolves, turned their attention to him, all conversations halting almost mid-word as he had to wait only a second for complete silence from his pack.

"We are here to rectify an egregious error made by one of our lesser wolves." My father didn't need to raise his voice to be heard. He turned to look at the younger wolf, who shied under the Alpha's direct attention. "One who has yet to earn a rightful place in our pack. One who dared to stand up against one of our dominant wolves." His tone sharpened. "If he desires to have a voice in the pack, then let him fight for that honor."

The color drained from the young wolf's face as the words fell over the crowd. He looked ready to pee his pants.

"This is bullshit," I hissed. A hand on my arm stopped me from saying anything else.

"Don't, V." My mother's voice was softer than mine, but still a few of the wolves near us turned curious glances our way.

"This isn't right."

"No, it isn't," she said, "but it's the way things are."

Sinclair stepped farther into the circle and the crowd began to murmur. His opponent did the same. I wished I knew the kid's name. He was one of the younger crowd, the ones that didn't get to spend much time with the dominants of the pack. He was lumped in with the submissives, even if that wasn't the kind of person he was.

I shook my head. This whole system was a crock of shit. I hated it.

But there was nothing I could do to stop what was about to happen. As the first blows fell, I turned away, walking to one of the nearby pillars and leaning against it. The downside to amplified werewolf hearing? I heard every blow that landed, every yip and grunt and growl, as a powerful werewolf beat a youngling to within an inch of his life.

"This is bullshit," I repeated under my breath.

"It is the way of things." My mother's voice made me jump. I glanced up to find her standing beside me, her back to the crowd who had started shouting and cheering. "It has been the way of things for a long time. We cannot simply change it."

"Why not? The world is changing, why can't we?"

"Because wolves have lived like this for centuries. Many of us are at least a century old. It will be a younger generation that changes things."

I kicked the pillar and knocked a chip of concrete off with my steel-toed boots. "How? The birth rate for wolves is low enough as it is. Without new Alphas there is no one to take over packs who hasn't already been indoctrinated into this bullshit. We need to start changing now!"

Whatever she was about to say in response was cut off by a loud howl followed by a roaring cheer from the watchers. I couldn't stand there anymore.

Without waiting for any sort of permission, I pushed my way through the crowd to the edge of the ring. My father stood in his spot, watching the display as the wolves around him jostled each other, but none came near him. In the middle of the makeshift ring was the young man, covered in bloody gashes and claw marks, still fully human. Standing over him with one arm raised was Sinclair, wearing nothing but a pair of jeans and covered in fur along his arms and chest and up his neck. He must've done a partial shift at the beginning of the fight. His poor opponent wasn't strong enough to do that.

I opened my mouth to shout for the fight to stop before

Sinclair could kill the kid, when suddenly the younger fighter leapt backward, just as Sinclair's claws slashed the air he'd occupied the moment before. He landed on his hands and knees, then managed one of the fastest shifts I'd ever seen. A second later there was a large dark-furred wolf on all fours growling at the Enforcer.

Whatever hope the kid's maneuver had put in my heart quickly faded when it was clear he still wasn't a match for the dominant wolf. Sinclair didn't bother to shift fully to fight. He stayed partially shifted and used his claws and fangs to terrifying effect. The sudden shift gained the kid more time, but it only served to draw out the inevitable.

Then a kick from Sinclair's boot caught the wolf hard in the side. He sailed through the air over the heads of the spectators, smashed against the concrete ceiling of the parking garage, then smacked into the ground. He twitched, and almost looked like he was going to get up. A second later, Sinclair charged toward him.

"No!" I shouted, beating him by mere seconds and grasping his wrist before another blow could land. "It's over. You won."

I struggled to hold his hand away from me and the young wolf for a good few seconds before a hard voice echoed through the garage.

"Enough."

Sinclair immediately backed down and ripped his arm from my grasp. He took a step back, then reverted to human form, the rush of battle still glowing in his eyes.

I heard the heavy steps of the Alpha approach. Adding simply another slight to my list tonight, I turned my back on him and knelt beside the wolf who wasn't a wolf anymore. The young man was lying on the ground, dazed and sore, but whole, missing only his clothing.

"Are you okay?" I asked.

He nodded but didn't say anything. I held a hand out and he stared at it for a long moment, his eyes full of distrust.

"I'm V," I told him.

"I know." His voice was weak, tired, but his eyes bored into mine with a strength that couldn't be diminished by someone like Sinclair. He ignored my hand and pushed himself to his knees. His eyes flashed over my face before he lowered his head in submission. I clenched my hand in anger before realizing that someone was standing right behind me.

"Move." The voice did not come from my father but from Sinclair. I stood and faced him with a snarl.

"Not a chance."

"You spit on our traditions."

"Definitely."

"Sinclair. Valerie." I cringed at the use of my full name. Once more my father didn't need to raise his voice to freeze us in our tracks.

"It's V," I snarled, and gave my father the fullest force of my best glare.

Sinclair backed off a couple steps, lowering his head to our Alpha. I stared him down.

Father leaned over to my ear, speaking so softly I had trouble hearing him. "Continue to disrespect me and there will be consequences, daughter."

"I'm not your *daughter*," I said, equally quiet. But I still took a step back and took on a less challenging posture. I wasn't about to grovel to the man, but he was my Alpha. As his child, I could only get away with so much.

"We will discuss this—and your position in the pack— later." He turned and clapped a hand on Sinclair's shoulder. The two men walked back toward the crowd of wolves, who started cheering for their champion. Sinclair played into it, throwing his arms in the air and roaring wildly.

"Fuck," I said under my breath. I turned back to the young man and found two other wolves there with him. Both young, both female, and both exactly what my father would call submissives. "And you are?"

"Friends," one of the girls said, "we'll take care of Cale. You can go celebrate with the rest of your kind."

I shook my head, reeling inwardly at the anger in her tone. "They aren't my kind."

The anger on the girl's face flickered. "If that's true, why work so hard to be one of them?"

"Because I want my own life. I won't be labeled a submissive and given to the first suitor my father chooses."

She scoffed. "That's our lot in life, why should you be any different?"

"Because I want that all to change. We need to do better. To be better."

"It's what every pack is like."

"There has to be a pack somewhere that works differently."

"If you find one, let us know," she said sarcastically. "In the meantime, this is all we have."

"I want to find a way that we can change it."

"How? You're not an Alpha."

I glanced at my father's back. "Trust me, I know." One of my greatest failings, according to him, was that I wasn't an Alpha. I wouldn't be the one to take over the pack from him someday. All other attempts thus far to have another child had failed. I was their one, and only, disappointment.

"Why did you help me?" Cale had found his voice as the women helped him to his feet.

"Don't talk to her," one of the girls said.

I shook my head. "I didn't want another dead wolf to bury." Oh yeah, that was also part of my job as Knight sometimes.

"Is that it?" he asked.

I sighed. "And the way we do things is wrong. The way the pack works is wrong. I want it to change. But sometimes it seems like I'm the only one."

"You aren't," he said.

The girls each took him by an arm and started half-walking, half-dragging him away.

I let them go without arguing. They didn't need to stick around and listen to Sinclair announcing his victory at the top of his lungs. In fact, I didn't feel the need to stick around for it either. I shot a glance at my father, but he seemed too busy with the adoring dominants of our pack to bother looking my way. My mother was somewhere in the crowd too, probably with a smile on her face that didn't reach her eyes.

Fuck it. They didn't need me here. If they wanted to talk, they could call. I left as quietly as I had arrived, jogging to the stairs and taking them two at a time to the ground floor of the parking structure. I kept moving quickly until I reached my motorcycle—a Honda CB500F, the pride of my life—and climbed on. I shivered as I revved up the engine and peeled out of the parking spot, headed home. I knew I hadn't escaped the consequences of my actions tonight, but at least I could put them out of my head for the ride home.

Which is exactly what I did.

CHAPTER THREE

Heather

I pulled a couple of shirts from the closet and folded them over my arm before shoving them unceremoniously into my duffel bag. I had no idea how long I'd be there, but honestly, I didn't want to spend too long away.

"I don't like this," Wren said. She was the nicest Alpha ever. She'd driven me back to the motel room that had been my home for the past eight months. But I hadn't exactly invited her in to watch me pack.

"I don't have a choice. It's my mom. I need to go."

"It's the mother who paid a witch to curse you in the first place. You don't owe her anything."

I shook my head. "I know that. I think I know that." I pulled out some more clothing to shove in the bag, but stopped and sat on the bed. I racked my brain to find the words to make my Alpha understand why I needed to do this. Why it couldn't wait. "I need to do this, Wren."

"But the first night of the full moon is tomorrow."

"I know." The nights right before and right after the full moon were just as dangerous for a young wolf as the particular night itself. For someone like me, those three nights were the only time my wolf deigned to make an appearance.

"You need to be somewhere your wolf is familiar with. You're still having too much trouble communicating and controlling her," Wren continued.

"You don't think I know that? You don't think I see you and Nat every day communicating with your wolves, making this shit look so damned easy, when I can't even feel her inside me? She doesn't talk to me! She doesn't want anything to do with me!"

"That's not true. You shifted when you came to look for me, and when I was taken you managed a partial shift! You can't do that if you're not in tune with your wolf."

"Joke's on you," I muttered. "She hasn't reared her head since then. We shift on the full moon, and you know that I can't remember what happens or where we go. All I can remember are snippets of a dream, like I'm asleep through it all."

"Give it time. It'll get better."

"I've given it eight months, Wren. If it was going to happen, it would have happened already. My wolf hates me, okay? She hates me because of what I put her through. Because I allowed her to be locked in a fucking cage for twenty-three years and now she holds a fucking grudge!"

"It wasn't your fault."

That clearly doesn't matter! I wanted to yell but instead clamped my mouth shut after my tirade. Wren didn't deserve to get yelled at like this. I couldn't handle it anymore. I needed to figure a way out of this. I needed to find a way to get my wolf to communicate with me. Otherwise it felt like nothing had changed, like I still had a piece of me inside that I couldn't explain, couldn't touch. Like I was half a person.

I never wanted to feel like that again.

"I know," I said, when I felt like my temper had simmered down enough that I could keep my voice to a rational level. "I know it wasn't my fault. But that doesn't seem to matter to my wolf. She blames me. I thought maybe…" I drifted off.

"Maybe?" Wren prompted.

I sighed. "Maybe if I could confront my mother, get some sort of closure, maybe I could make something work with my wolf. Maybe it would give her a chance to work with me. I don't know. Maybe I'm dreaming."

Wren bit her lip like she wasn't sure what she wanted to say next. I closed my eyes, trying to calm myself and the itchiness I'd been feeling just under my skin since I'd gotten the phone call in the first place.

You need to come home.

Those were words I'd never thought I'd hear from anyone in my family. I was told never to come back, after I had argued with my mother that night and chosen to leave. Summer had been there too, always on Mother's side. I was a monster. A freak, an abomination. Even before I knew what I was, I was looked at like the mistake, like an outsider. Summer was the perfect daughter. The golden child. She could do no wrong, and her father had been entirely human.

I didn't remember ever meeting my father. He was out of the picture before I was born. Was he part of the local pack in Edmonton? I had no idea. All I knew was that my mother had been in love and gotten pregnant before he revealed what he was to her. It was too much for her to take. She drove him away, but carried the baby anyway. She said that it was early when she realized that I was just like him. That she went searching for someone who could give me what she called a normal life. So I wouldn't be a monster.

It was torture, growing up like there was a piece missing. Like I wasn't a whole person. No matter how much I said that something was off, I was told otherwise. I was always wrong in how I felt. I learned early to second-guess everything I was feeling, everything that I was thinking, because I didn't want someone to tell me that what I was feeling or thinking was wrong. That kind of constant second-guessing destroys a child's confidence in themselves.

It certainly destroyed mine.

"I get it." Wren's voice made me jump and my eyes snapped open. She was kneeling in front of me, the look on her face so damned caring that I almost wanted to cry. "I get why you want to do this, and it could be the last time you get the chance. I just don't want anything to happen to you."

"Thank you, Alpha." I lowered my head, less in submission and more in weariness. "If I had any other choice, I wouldn't be doing this. But I don't."

"I understand. And I wish I could come with you."

"Not a chance. Natalie needs you here and you need her just as badly. She's not ready to shift in a big city like Edmonton." I put a hand on her shoulder. "I'm only a few hours away. I'll be okay."

"I know. I know it. I don't want you to go."

"It's not like I'm going back to Winnipeg. I'm not going back to the Cardinals. This is a city with a pack that doesn't know us, doesn't know what we've been through. I'll do the right thing. I'll visit my mother first thing when I get there and then see the Alpha in the morning. I won't step on anyone's toes. I promise."

"I'm not worried about that. If someone tries to hurt a member of my pack, I will make them pay, I don't care who they are or what pack they're with." A growl started low in her throat, and I resisted the urge to back away farther onto the bed. "I'm worried about you not being able to control your shifts for the next three nights."

"I'll find a safe spot to shift. I promise." I stood from

the bed and continued packing my duffel. Wren continued to watch me while I did so. It didn't take long to finish, though, and as I headed toward the door she followed.

"Take the sedan," she said, her voice commanding. She held out a small ring of keys. "You're comfortable driving it, right? I know you've borrowed it a couple times."

"Yeah, not so much on the highway, but I'll make it work." I reached out for the keys but she didn't let go.

"Take care of yourself, wolf," she said, her voice low like she was warning me against something. "I won't hesitate to come after you if you get in trouble."

"I understand, Alpha."

She let go of the keys and they fell into my palm.

"Good luck, Heather."

I leaned in and gave my Alpha a hug, then headed for the sedan. It was a model from the mid-nineties but still ran fine, even if it did guzzle gas a little bit too much for my liking. I drove away from the motel and headed for the highway back toward the city. Wren's Jeep followed behind me until she had to turn the opposite direction to head back to her cabin and her engagement party. My heart sank. I'd taken her away from what was supposed to be a happy occasion. Just one more way I'd gone and screwed up someone else's life. Classic Heather. Making things more difficult for everyone.

I shook my head. That was the kind of shit I was trying to get over. The self-pity, the negative self-talk. The kind of stuff a therapist would charge way too much to tell me to change but not give me any actual way to do such a thing. It's all in my mind, they would say. I'd have to work to change it. There were no shortcuts. There wasn't a single way to do these things.

I hated therapists, but most of all, I hated that they were right.

The three-hour drive was filled with bland music and a ton of self-doubt. This wasn't the best idea. Wren was right about that. The itching under my skin only got worse and worse as I got closer to the city. I couldn't decide if it was because I was about to see my mother again for the first time since I ran away to Winnipeg, or if it was my wolf feeling nervous about being in the city that had cursed us in the first place.

Who does that to a child? Adults who think they know better, obviously. Adults who think they know everything, and their child is just a child who has no idea about what's happening to them, or that they might be different than their parent wants them to be.

I shook my head and wiped my eyes before the tears could blur my vision too much. This was not the time to be thinking about all that. I had to focus on the road.

I might have been gone for a while, but I still knew the roads around the city like the back of my hand. Summer had called from the University Hospital, and that's where I headed immediately. The traffic was light at this time of night, and it didn't take long to find a spot in the lot. I paid for parking for the rest of the day—it's ridiculous to force people to pay to visit their sick loved ones—and ran in the front door.

The smell of the hospital was the first thing to hit me, and I froze in my steps. Antibacterial cleanliness mixed with the scent of fear and illness and sadness, and everything else mixed into a cacophony of smells that almost made me lose the dinner I'd eaten back at the party. I girded myself and pressed forward, heading toward the front desk. A world-weary nurse looked up from her computer, standing between me and my goal.

"I'm sorry, ma'am, but visiting hours are—"

"I just got into town. My mother is in the ICU. I need to see her."

She gave a long-suffering sigh. "Name?"

"Cecily McKenna."

She tapped in a few things on the keyboard, then picked up the phone. I waited as patiently as I could, resisting the urge to scratch long furrows into my arms to alleviate that itching under my skin.

Settle down, I told myself. Well, told my wolf, really. Whether or not she heard me was anyone's guess.

"Yeah, Trish? Can you come down and escort someone up? Her mother is up there," the nurse said tersely into the handset. "I know. I know. Just do it, please." She hung up and turned back to me. "A nurse will be down to escort you up. You'll have a few minutes to see her, but you can't stay the night."

I shook my head. "That's no problem. I just got in and I really need to see her. Thank you. Thank you so much."

She gave me a wan smile as the elevator around the corner dinged. "It's what we do."

A few seconds later a tall blonde wearing loose scrubs and comfortable shoes power-walked around the corner. She gave each of us a long look, then crooked her finger toward me. "ICU?"

I nodded.

"This way, please."

We rode the elevator in silence, Trish tapping away on her phone as her brow furrowed. She led me to another nurse's desk that was empty. She slipped behind the computer.

"Name?" she asked. I gave it to her and held my breath, waiting to be told something horrible. Instead she pointed to the blue line on the floor. "Follow that line, room three-oh-five. I think there's already someone in there with her."

"I think my sister is here."

"We can't let you two stay all night, but we can give you a

little time." She gave me a small smile like she knew what we were going through, and I appreciated the moment of empathy so much. I scratched at my arm and said thanks, then followed the blue line. It didn't take long to find the room.

I faltered, scratching at my arm again. I had to look like I was on something, the amount of scratching I was doing up and down my arm. The thin white lines were starting to turn red and it was only a matter of time before I managed to puncture the skin, though any gashes wouldn't last long with my werewolf physiology. I stared at the door for a long moment. I didn't want my family to see me like this. They already thought I was a monster. Hell, I *was* a monster. But this would be the first time I'd seen them since that night over four years ago. If I hadn't kept my phone, Summer probably never would have found me, and I wouldn't know that my mom was sick.

I shook my head. This was ridiculous. I needed to see my mother to fix what was broken between us? I was a grown-ass woman. I had been through so much, despite still being a young adult. But I knew if I could see her, talk to her, get through to her maybe, that it could change how my wolf and I communicated. It would let my wolf see that I wanted her to be a part of me, that we were meant to be together.

I was stronger than this. I was stronger than them. I could handle this. Couldn't I?

"Heather?"

The sound of my name jolted me into action. As much as I wanted to turn and leave, instead I stepped into the room where my sister was waiting, watching me as I entered. Summer ran forward, wrapped her arms tightly around me, and thrust her head into my collarbone with a soft wail. She was slightly smaller than me with hair a shade or two lighter than my own. I remembered how well we fit together as she clung to me. It reminded me of the better times of my childhood—the few that there were.

"I can't believe you're actually here." Her voice was muffled against my shirt, and I resisted the urge to peel her off of me.

Certainly not the welcome I was expecting.

I managed to get my arms to work and held my younger sister awkwardly as I patted her back.

"Of course I'm here."

"I wasn't sure you'd come."

"I…" I was about to say that I wasn't a monster, but that wasn't true. "I had to come. How is she?"

Summer pulled herself off me and stepped back, giving the barest of glances to the bed in the center of the room like she couldn't stand to look at it.

"I don't know, I couldn't understand anything the doctor was saying. But she's been unconscious since this afternoon. She's breathing, so I guess that's a good thing, but she won't wake up."

I looked from her to the bed. Cecily McKenna lay there, looking far older than I remembered from the last time I saw her. I scratched my arm as I moved closer. Here was the woman who had all but destroyed my life. The woman who made me doubt everything about myself. The woman who said I was wrong every time I told her I felt different from everyone else. The one who pushed me to be normal even though I felt like I never would be. The one who punished me when I didn't conform to her wishes.

The itching under my skin got worse and I scratched harder, leaving furrows that drew small amounts of blood before quickly closing again. My nails weren't made of silver; my body had no problem healing such small wounds quickly.

But Summer didn't know that.

"What the hell?" she all but screeched, as if she remembered at the last minute to keep her voice down in the hospital. I spun around to see her staring at the arm that I continued to scratch.

"What—" I began, then looked at my arm too. There was fur starting to grow up and down it, emerging and receding as if it were following my fingers and the direction of the scratches. Suddenly, as if seeing it triggered something inside me, the itching became exponentially worse and started all over my body. I cried out and backed away from the hospital bed. I held my arm as I tried to fight back whatever it was that was happening to me.

"I thought you were fixed!" Summer hissed at me, and her words were filled with the vitriol I was used to from my family. "I thought you went away to fix yourself! Fix your curse!"

"I did." I ground my teeth against the itching. I tried to focus on my breathing so I wouldn't end up shifting right there and then. That was the last thing I needed. "My wolf is free now. I'm free of the curse our mother had put on me."

"She did it so you'd have a normal life! So you could be human!"

"But I'm not human," I said, "and I never was. I'm finally fully myself." *Even if I can't really control what happens to me*, I added silently.

"Then what's going on?"

I shook my head. "I don't know. I'm trying not to shift but it's hard. It's strong emotions and—" I took a deep breath through my nose and picked up all the scents from the room and beyond: Summer's fear, my mother's illness, and that overly clean smell of the hospital. I hissed in pain as fur grew again on my arm, but I couldn't let the change happen. It didn't take long to realize my wolf was making herself known and didn't care what I thought about it at all.

Summer's eyes went wide, and she moved toward the door. She did not glance back before she was gone.

I needed to control this. I hadn't had an unplanned shift in months. Here, now, with my mother in the bed and Summer running away was not the time for this shit to happen again. I needed to stop this.

I backed myself into the far corner, pushing back against my wolf. I didn't want to. I wanted her to know that we could communicate, work together. But now wasn't a good time to change. I wouldn't have any control if we did. I needed to be in control right now—at least until we found somewhere to shift and go for a run. I tried to send all these thoughts and feelings to my wolf, but nothing stopped the worsening itching and pain that came through as the fur started to stick around longer and longer every time it jutted out from my arm.

"No!"

CHAPTER FOUR

V

I had just brought the bike to a stop in my assigned parking stall when my phone buzzed in my back pocket. I sighed. This late at night it could only mean one of two things—either I was in trouble or I needed to handle something. Given what had happened tonight, I was probably in trouble. I leaned back on the bike, cradled it between my legs, and checked the message.

Fuck.

It was from my mother. My father was none too graciously demanding my presence. At their house. Right away.

Of course he was using her as a go-between. If he'd messaged me himself I'd have probably completely ignored it. But because it came from her, I was torn. I could pretend that I was already home and asleep by the time I got the message, and go in the morning. And that was probably the better idea so I didn't confront my father when I was feeling in such a contrary mood.

But.

The Alpha said right away, and you don't defy the Alpha. Despite my attitude toward him tonight, I couldn't straight-out defy him. So against my own better judgment I put the bike in gear and took off.

My parents lived in the river valley, on the north shore in a little community called Riverdale. A lot of the pack lived down there, the ones that could afford houses, anyway. They had lived in the area for most of the city's life, since first coming here. Despite the city's continual growth, the wilder areas remained untouched save for walking trails through some of the parks. Perfect for a citybound werewolf.

It didn't take long for me to go across the river and into their community. My bike was the only vehicle on the roads this late, most of the houses darkened for the night. I parked on the street in front of a particularly nice house, three floors of delusions of grandeur and childhood nightmares. They'd expanded the house multiple times, buying the lots around them when they went up for sale, to fit what they had hoped would be a large family. But no, there was only me, and I had left the house as early as I could manage it. Now as far as I knew they housed other pack members who didn't have another place to go for whatever reason. Though that was mostly my mother's doing. My father couldn't care less, but didn't stop her. He wasn't a brute, after all.

Still, I avoided coming here as much as I could. Too many rough memories.

I parked my bike on the street and slowly made my way up the walk. The door opened and my mother appeared, beckoning me forward like a lighthouse beacon—one I didn't want to follow. But I did it anyway.

"Whatever happens," she said as I reached the doorway and she took my arm, "whatever he says, just agree. It will be easier."

"What are you talking about?"

"I'm sorry. You cut it too close tonight. He's angry. Irrational. Just stay calm and I'll work on him."

"Has he done something to you?"

She shook her head. "No, no, nothing like that. You know he wouldn't dare." She pulled me through the foyer and toward the study where dear old Dad loved to have his important discussions. She lowered her voice as we moved, like she didn't want him to overhear. "He's going to say some things that you don't like. I need you to work with him, okay? I promise, whatever happens I will help make it go away, but if you rile him up further I won't be able to do that. Do you understand?"

"No, I don't understand! What the hell is going on? What does he want?" As punctuation to my words the study door opened and my father openly glared the moment his eyes fell on me. I gave him my sweetest smile and pulled my arm out of my mother's grip. She fell silent under my father's gaze as he swept an arm sideways.

"Valerie." I shivered with the coldness in his tone. As much as I wanted to correct him, Mother's warnings echoed in my head and I let this one go. For now.

I walked past him into the study. It was a large room with a high, vaulted ceiling. A large bookshelf sat behind a heavy, ornate desk and was filled to the brim with leather tomes and newer paperbacks. I ached to get in there and rearrange it to piss him off, but now was not the time. There were chairs around his desk that he used to talk business, but there was also a more informal sitting area that I headed for immediately. I took a seat on a small couch that was bought for its looks, not its comfort, and leaned back against it, throwing an arm out and trying to look as at ease as I could manage. I stifled a yawn. It was late already and I still had to make the ride home.

He closed the door lightly and turned toward me with a look in his eyes that screamed self-control. This wasn't my father, the man who tried to raise me in what he thought was the best way. No, this was Desmond Raines, Alpha of the Raines pack of Edmonton.

"We need to discuss what happened tonight." His words lacked the fire of anger that I expected to hear from him, and I straightened up on the couch. Mother's words were starting to make more sense. I'd pushed him too far. "You challenged me in front of the pack. You challenged Sinclair. You challenged everything that makes this pack what it is."

"I—"

He cut me off with a look. "You disparage our culture, everything that we do. There are reasons that we run packs the way that we do. It keeps us strong, able to weather anything that may come to destroy us. We survived the calamity so long ago by adopting this pack structure. It works. It is not to be changed."

"It's barbaric."

"Life is often barbaric. Survival in its purest form is barbaric. Strong wolves make a strong pack. Those strong wolves are kept happy by the Alpha offering the weaker wolves to them. This keeps the strong wolves in the pack and keeps our pack strong. That is the truth of things."

"Why are you telling me all of this?"

"I am trying to make you understand why you cannot do what you did tonight." He let out a large sigh. "And why I am forced to do what comes next."

"What are you talking about?"

He looked at me with a coldness I never thought would be directed toward his only child. "You will mate bond with Sinclair. It will be announced on the second night of the full moon before the pack run."

"What the f—" I drew myself up from the couch, barely able to believe what he'd said.

"You brought this on yourself, daughter of mine. Your disgust for our practices and the way we run things needs to change. Sinclair will help with that. Also, having two strong wolves mated will increase the chance that you will bear an Alpha and I will have a proper successor."

"Fuck you! I won't do it."

"Yes, you will." It didn't matter how loud I got, he continued speaking in that cold, emotionless tone. "You don't understand, child. You have no choice in the matter. It has been decided."

"And I don't get a say in it?"

"Not after your actions tonight, no."

"This is fucking bullshit."

"You brought it on yourself!" He finally lost his cool. "You have sneered at everything that I try to do for this pack, everything that we represent. Now you'll learn the hard way why we do what we do. What we have to do to keep this pack strong so no one else tries to take our territory from us. Or worse, our pack."

I scoffed. "The last pack war in these parts was so long ago only the oldest of us can remember it. Are you really scared that someone is going to try something?"

"We must always be on guard! There was an attack on a pack west of here just last year. It still happens, but not to a pack that is strong and works together."

I crossed my arms, knowing I looked and sounded like a petulant child, but it was better than the alternative. "I don't care about any of that. I'm not mating with Sinclair in any way, shape, or form. I flat-out refuse."

"You are going to do this."

"You know I like women! I have been honest with you

about being sapphic, about being nonbinary. How can you possibly think I would agree to this?"

"Because I thought you would see what is best for the pack, not just for yourself. I do not remember raising you to be so selfish."

"*Selfish?*" I clenched my fists. "It's *selfish* to be myself? To be the person that I am and who I want to be? To care about myself and not want to be attached to a disgusting brute of a man for the next two centuries?"

"You are my daughter, and you will do what is good for the pack."

I shook my head. "You don't see what you're doing to your pack, do you? How the young wolves hate being a part of what you've built. That tonight you allowed one of your strongest wolves to beat a wolf who hasn't even come of age in a pitched fight!"

"Everything I do is for the good of the pack. You would do well to remember that, daughter."

"I won't do it. Pick one of your submissives to mate with the asshole."

"I have chosen you. That is the end of this discussion."

I opened my mouth to continue arguing when my phone buzzed loudly. Desmond looked at me expectantly and I snarled. I pulled the phone out and checked it.

"It's Trish at the University Hospital," I said. "9-1-1. Got a possible rogue wolf."

"Then go take care of it, my Knight."

I glared at him. "This conversation is not over. I refuse to mate with Sinclair."

"If you do not, there will be consequences."

I was about to ask him what those might be but decided I probably didn't want to know. I snarled another curse at him and stormed out of the study. I passed my mother without a word and headed back to my bike. I kicked it into gear and sped off into the night once more, still chewing on the words I hadn't said.

By the time I got to the hospital all I wanted to do was go home and sleep. Instead, I parked the bike in the short-term lot, paid the stupid money for a parking pass, then headed for the doors.

Then a scent hit my nose and my wolf surged forward, trying to wrest control from me in a way they hadn't done in years.

"Easy," I murmured. I paused and took in the scent again. Whatever it was, it made my wolf excited and wild, and I didn't know how else to describe it. It took a third sniff for it to really hit me.

It was the scent of spring rains, of an apple freshly bitten into, of the most succulent of meats being grilled on the barbecue. It was every smell I'd ever loved all rolled into one intangible, beautiful scent.

I followed it to a nearby old-model sedan. A few sniffs around it and the scent was permanently burned into my brain, a smell I would never, ever forget. Who was this wolf? And why were they driving this old heap of scrap? I needed to find them and make sure they knew that I would take care of them, that I would find a better vehicle for them to drive and make sure they'd be happy and healthy and—

What the fuck?

I shook my head. That was…weird. I focused and headed for the front doors, letting them slide open to reveal that scent again, fainter this time, tinged with the chemical smell of hospital. I tuned out the hospital scent and followed the other past the front desk, ignored the overworked nurse and headed for the elevators. She didn't try to stop me.

The scent was in the elevator too. I wanted to bathe in it, to rub my face against the wolf who was giving off this scent. *Okay, come on, V, relax.* I needed to focus on what I was doing. This scent was enticing, intoxicating, and it was going to make it harder to do what I needed to do. If this was the rogue wolf that Trish had called me here for…

The elevator doors opened, and I stepped out—almost into the arms of a young woman. We dodged each other at the last second and she spun into the elevator behind me. I caught her scent and frowned. She had the scent on her, but it was weak, it didn't originate from her. The doors closed as I stared at her, meeting her icy eyes for only a second. Fear. Panic. Something around here had scared the shit out of her.

"V!"

I spun away from the elevator and found Trish coming around the corner like she'd been following the woman.

"Hey, Trish."

Trish was one of a few wolves we had working at the hospital. She worked the night shift a lot and could help us find wolves who might've been brought in under the assumption that they were human. This was the first time she'd called in about a possible rogue wolf in our territory.

"I'm glad you came," she said, walking quickly toward me. "I don't know who she is, but she came to see her mom."

"Her mom?"

"A human."

I stopped for a second. That was rare. It was hard enough for werewolves to have children with each other. The oldest of us said it was a punishment from the Mother of Wolves. My guess was it was something genetic, but what did I know? A human giving birth to a wolf was all but unheard of. It took at least one werewolf to make another, so if her mother was human...

"Walk and talk," I said, throwing an arm around her shoulder and heading down the hallway, keeping in mind that we were following the path of that ever-so-enticing scent.

"She came in about twenty minutes ago. I texted you as soon as I realized she was a wolf. I didn't recognize her at all and she didn't smell like anyone from the pack."

"Doesn't sound like she's here for something nefarious."

"No, but it's my job to inform the pack of any abnormalities."

I smiled at her. "You did good, I'm not criticizing. Just... curious is all." I took another sniff of that glorious scent. "Did she smell...different to you?"

"Different? Like how?"

I shook my head. "Never mind."

"No!"

The cry echoed sharply through the hallways. We glanced at each other for only a second before we started running.

"Was that her?"

"I think so," Trish said. "What's going on?"

"I don't know, but I need you to stay put and make sure no one interferes. Can you do that?"

"What are you going to do?"

I wasn't sure at this point, but said, "What I'm supposed to."

I didn't give her a chance to ask more questions as I followed my nose to the room where I knew I would find this wolf. My wolf pushed me forward faster than I should move in public, they were so intent on finding the source of the amazing scent. Like a cartoon skunk drifting on air after the perfume of an unlucky cat, my wolf almost felt like they were going into heat. This was getting ridiculous, but I couldn't argue with them when I was feeling the same way. I was just able to control it better.

I slipped into the room without caring what number it was and found two people. The first was an older woman lying in the bed, hooked up to a plethora of machines. I had no idea what most of them did but assumed they were good for her. The other was a younger woman, curled almost into the fetal position in the far corner of the room. Her eyes flashed up to me and she let out a cry, picking herself up enough to sit up and put her arms out.

"Don't!" she said. "Don't come any closer. Please!"

I raised my hands slowly. "It's okay. I'm here to help."

"Get away!"

I shook my head. "I can't do that."

"You're not a nurse!"

I glanced down at my jeans and leather jacket. "Nope. Not a nurse. But I can help you, and you know it. You and your wolf."

She stared for a long second, and I saw fur sprout along one arm briefly before it receded. Shit. This girl was fighting a change. Meanwhile, on the inside my wolf was going wild and battering against the mental blocks that helped keep me from shifting whenever the wolf wanted. Damn, did they want to right now.

"You're here to kill me?" she asked. It almost sounded like a plea.

"Not if I can help it. In my line of work killing is a last resort, thank you."

"I'm a wolf who can't control her shifting. I know how packs work." She tensed as the fur appeared on both arms, then receded as she closed her eyes and took a long, stuttering breath.

"You seem to be controlling it fine right now."

"You call this fine?"

Deciding it was safe enough if she was willing to banter with me, I moved forward. She tried to press herself farther into the corner.

"Stay away! Please! I can't hurt anyone. I won't let her."

I moved closer despite her protests. About a foot from her, I crouched down to look her in the eye.

"I won't let you or your wolf hurt anyone. I promise."

"How can you promise that? You don't know me!"

I took a long sniff of the air and my eyes almost rolled to the back of my head in pleasure. This was her. She was mine. My mate. My fated mate.

I shook my head. "I don't know you, but I plan to change that. You have no idea what kind of wonderful timing you have. Truly, you've saved my life."

She stared at me like I was speaking nonsense, and I leaned back a little, confused. Did she not feel it too? I watched her cringe again and saw fur appear on her face then disappear. She was still fighting the change. And fighting it hard.

"Come on," I said, holding my arms out to her, "I can take you somewhere safe."

"Why should I trust you? I don't even know who you are!"

"I'm V," I said. I smiled and slipped into my usual casual introduction, "I'm nonbinary. I use they/them pronouns. I'm the Knight for the Raines clan. My father is the Alpha. What else do you want to know?"

She stared at me like I had two heads, and I offered my arms again. She took them slowly, cringing as my bare hands touched the fur on her arms that wasn't receding as fast as it had been.

"Heather…is me," she said softly, allowing me to pull her up. I worried about how easy it was to pull her up. She was far too light under the ill-fitting sundress she was wearing. "Please, don't let me hurt anyone. I don't want to be a monster."

I resisted the urge to flinch at the way she said *monster*. The term got thrown around a lot about werewolves, but the way she said it made me wonder who had ingrained it into her so deeply that she truly thought she was monstrous.

"Oh, honey," I said, pulling her into my arms for a quick moment. "You're beautiful."

I pulled her along with me, out of the room and past Trish, who was still guarding the doorway. I didn't acknowledge her. Instead I focused solely on Heather and getting her out of the hospital before she lost control. On the main floor, as we headed for the doors, the desk nurse stood as if to stop us and I shook my head at her.

"She couldn't handle seeing her mom like that," I said softly, earning a sympathetic smile. "We'll be back tomorrow."

We slipped out through the doors and into the cold air. I pulled her away from the parking lot, forgoing the cars, and headed north as quickly as we could manage. A nearby copse of trees was thick enough to hide in for the moment, so I stopped and pulled her against me once more as I resisted my wolf's urge to take her and mate with her right here and now.

Easy, my wolf, not yet.

"If you follow me, we can run from here to the river valley. We'll be safe there."

Heather shook her head. "I don't know. I can't control her. She makes her own decisions."

That makes things easier.

I was pretty certain that her wolf would follow my wolf anywhere—mostly because right now I knew mine would follow hers.

"Trust me, please." I cupped her face in my hands and

couldn't help myself. I pressed my lips against hers, taking a little taste of what I hoped would be mine.

If her smell was glorious, her taste was absolutely divine. Better than the finest dishes I'd ever eaten, but simple and clean and something I would never, ever forget.

She pulled back a little, her face flushed and her eyes wild. "Why did you do that?"

"Because I was desperate to taste you," I said honestly.

Her mouth dropped open and fur erupted over most of her body like she had abruptly forgotten to stop fighting it. She cried out and dropped to all fours, unable to stop the change when it was so far gone. I knelt down next to her, placing my hand on her head.

"We're meant to be together," I said, "mates, you and me. We're mates, and you showed up at the perfect time."

By the time I was done talking she had fully shifted into her wolf form. Immediately, the beast tried to bowl me over, tongue frantically licking my skin as if also seeking a taste of me. I laughed and pushed her off, retrieving the loose sundress that had fallen off her wolf body and folding it nicely.

"Are you going to follow me?" I asked the wolf. "I know a safe place to put our clothes, and we can run for a while."

The wolf snorted at me. I took that as a yes. I ran my hands through her long fur and led us out of the trees and off into the wild areas of the city.

CHAPTER FIVE

Heather

I opened my eyes to a soft autumn light filtering through tall trees. I was lying on a bed of leaves on the floor of a wild forest. The foliage was all the colors of fall, with reds and yellows and browns, and even stubborn greens. The light came from above, the source hidden by the distant canopy. I sat up and glanced around, but there was nothing but trees and shrubs and undergrowth. I realized a second later that I was naked but not cold, as if the ambient air was warm and cozy and could almost lull a person to sleep. Almost.

"Where am I?" It was early spring and there was no way anywhere in Canada had these kinds of colors right now. And the daytime? The last thing I remembered was feeling V's lips on mine. That surprise kiss was the most beautiful thing I'd ever tasted. Made that kiss from the were-kitty so long ago seem like a peck on the cheek.

"Hello?" I called out, thinking that someone might hear me. But there was no response save for a soft rustling of foliage in an invisible wind that I didn't feel. Chills ran down my spine as I realized where I was.

A dreamscape. That's what Wren and Natalie had called it. They told me about the dreams they'd shared last year, about dark woods with tall trees where they could be together and communicate, even if they weren't close by.

But why now? Why was I here? Was this something to do with V? There were too many questions and no fucking answers and I hated it.

"Hey."

I spun around and saw V in front of me, also entirely naked and seemingly proud of it. And why not? They were a fucking specimen. There was a long winding tattoo of a vine with thorns and flowers that moved up their right leg, crossed over their hip, and continued upward toward their shoulder. Other tattoos adorned their left side—an ornate sword that looked like something out of The Legend of Zelda *on their upper left shoulder, and some cool-looking cyberpunk tech along their left forearm. Their raven-dark hair was cut short, barely falling to their neck while the right side had a shorn undercut to it. Their brown eyes stared at me and roamed up and down, as if taking in what they hadn't been able to see at the hospital.*

I shook myself out of my stupor and looked away. No matter how good they looked, I needed to know what the heck was going on.

"What is this?"

"Dunno. Never had this happen before."

"Are we asleep? Dead? What?"

"I don't think so. I think our wolves are in control. Least that's the last thing I remember."

"What? I can't let her be in control! She's going to hurt someone! I need to wake up, to shift back. I need—"

They moved toward me, took me into their strong arms, and I melted immediately. Brain fog stopped whatever else I was going to say.

"*Easy, easy,*" *they murmured.* "*It'll be okay. My wolf will take care of you. You will be okay.*"

I turned in their arms and stared at the lips that were at my eyeline. "*So this is a dream?*"

"*I guess you could look at it like that.*"

I watched their lips as they spoke, mesmerized by how red they were without having anything on them.

"*I usually ride along with my wolf, but I gave them the night this time, and then suddenly I'm here.*"

"*Lucky you,*" *I muttered.*

"*What's that?*"

I shook my head, feeling my face brush against their formidable—and beautiful—chest. My mouth was so close to one of their nipples and I longed to taste.

I pulled away and forced myself out of their arms. "*No. No, this isn't me. This isn't what I do.*"

They looked confused. "*What do you mean?*"

"*I'm not going to fawn over you just because you saved me at the hospital and now we're stuck in this dreamscape thing and I want to get down on my knees and have my way with you, but I'm not like that, and I'm not just going to run into this and get blindsided. I've had too much shit go wrong in my life to do that kind of thing, and I swear I am not just—*"

"*Whoa, whoa, whoa,*" *they said, raising their hands.* "*Slow down there, honey. I'm not asking you to fawn over me or anything.*"

"*Well, I'm not going to.*"

"*I understand. But you can't deny that we have some sort of connection. We wouldn't be here together if we didn't.*"

I snorted. "*I had a pretty good connection with a feline shifter some years ago too. Doesn't mean anything.*"

Their brow furrowed. "*Why are you so against this?*"

"Because I'm not ready for this! I don't know how to communicate with my wolf, and now you're here and I'm supposed to take it on faith that you're my mate? You're the one that I'm supposed to spend the next couple centuries with provided nothing bad happens and we don't die before that? I don't think I can handle this!"

They were silent for a long moment after my tirade.

"Am I not good enough to be your mate?" they asked softly.

Immediately, regret filled my entire soul. "No! No, not at all. That's not what I mean. I mean, you're gorgeous, and sexy, and fuck, I have a thing for tattoos, and I love yours! They look so damned good and I'm babbling again, and I can't seem to stop, and damn it you're perfect, but I don't deserve perfect!"

"Oh, honey, you deserve to have everything in the world."

"I don't! I really don't!" I wrapped my arms around myself and turned away from V, unable to continue looking at them. I didn't know them and I already had made a fool of myself. I was too much of a monster. Like my mother always said.

Then a second pair of arms was around me, and I sank into the embrace. V's arms were tight and warm and comforting. Everything that I didn't deserve.

"Please, V, don't," I whispered. "I can't do this. I can't make this happen. You deserve better than me."

"Maybe," they said, "maybe that is true. But who are you to decide what I deserve, huh?"

"Everyone deserves better than me."

"I only just met you, honey, and I already know that isn't true." Their voice was strong and even, like they meant what they were saying.

Their words were drilling through the barricades my mind was building, as fast as they were going up. Memories of my time with the Cardinal pack, being the lowest of the low, flooded my mind. Growing up with my mother, who always held the fact that I was different over my head, even when I didn't know why, had set me up for that.

"This is a dream," I said, "this isn't happening. This isn't real."

"I may not have all the answers, but this is real, Heather. All of this, you, me, this place. It's all real and it belongs to us."

They pressed their lips to the back of my neck, and I shivered under the touch. Those lips left a trail of kisses down my collarbone until I couldn't keep my moan in anymore. I turned and met their lips with mine and got lost for a moment in the intense bliss that the taste of them brought.

How had this happened? Why was I so intoxicated by this person? I knew that true mates were already predisposed to be attracted to each other, but honestly this felt like a little much, didn't it? Or was that my own insecurity telling me that I can't have something that I kind of desperately want, that it might not be good for either of us?

Why wouldn't it be good for V? Duh. I was a monster. I was a terrible excuse for a werewolf. Here was this perfect specimen of a wolf shifter from a strong pack who probably had a wonderful, cushy life there, and now I'd come along and messed it all up.

As for me, well, clearly, I was too broken for anyone to have. I knew it, logically, when I thought about things. A metric shit ton of mommy issues combined with the problems I had with my wolf and the simple idea of shifting, never mind actually trying to keep control of my wolf and making sure she didn't hurt someone.

All of that was getting thrown away for one more taste of those lips in this magical dream that I still couldn't be certain was some form of reality. I kissed them again and again, feeling that aching in my core that told me to do so much more. but I still hesitated. I dragged them down to my level, tasting every inch of their lips, down their cheek, their neck, their collarbone, until I nipped at the skin there as if marking them as mine.

I pulled away suddenly, almost afraid of what I'd been about to do.

"Heather, are you okay?"

Damn it. They sounded so damned patient, so polite. It was infuriating. I wanted them to get mad at me for being a tease, for leaving them wanting. Something, anything!

"No. No, I'm not. I'm sorry, but I don't know if I can do this."

"It's okay. We'll take it slow, okay? As slow as you need to go."

I stared at them. "Can you do that? Can you handle that?" Can you handle me? *was what I was really asking.*

"Yes, I can."

They said it with such surety that I couldn't help but believe them. I let them wrap their arms around me once more, and we lowered ourselves to the bed of leaves beneath our feet.

Time had no true meaning in this dreamscape, and we lay on the ground together until it became hard to keep my eyes open. They never once asked for any more than I was willing to give, and I was able to push my fears away for that splendid time, wrapped up in their arms.

When the dream finally disappeared in front of me, there was no panic, no fear. Only contentment.

I could get used to that.

CHAPTER SIX

Heather

Birdsong was the first thing I heard as I came awake in an unfamiliar setting. And next to an unfamiliar body, spooning me on the bed of grass and weeds and everything else that belongs on the floor of a forest that isn't in my dreams. For a long moment I curled into those strong arms, feeling safe for the first time in not-so-recent memory.

It didn't last.

I opened my eyes and kept them open, knowing that this little fantasy couldn't last. Reality was too good at getting in the way. I pulled out of V's arms—earning a grumble from them—and pulled myself to my feet. My very naked feet.

"Fuck." I managed not to scream it too loudly and draw attention to the fact that there were two naked people in the middle of the river valley. V stirred on the leaves as I looked around, desperate for something to wear. I caught sight of folded clothing on a large rock nestled in tree roots, what looked like V's leather jacket and pants and top sitting over my sundress I'd borrowed from Natalie. There was only one pair of boots, and I sighed, pretty sure I'd shifted out of mine the night before.

I grabbed the dress and started to pull it over my head,

then felt my shoulder twinge uncomfortably. I glanced at my collarbone, at the thin line of harsh-looking scabs in the shape of a wolf's bite staring back at me.

"What the fuck?" I shouted loudly enough to scare nearby animals out of their hiding places. The sound startled V, who threw themselves up to their feet and took a stance that looked ready for battle.

"What? What is it?"

"What the fuck did you do?"

"What are you talking about?"

I pointed at my shoulder, then at theirs, which had a matching scar. "You said we'd take it slow! You said that would be okay."

They held up their hands. "Heather, hold on a second. You need to calm down."

"Do not tell me to calm down!" I hated how much my voice had become a screech, but I couldn't help it. "You lied to me, V. You said we'd take it slow. Do you call *this* slow?"

They stared at me for a long moment, then glanced down at their own collarbone, at their own mate bite. Because that's what it was. It was clear as day. Sometime last night we bit each other with the magic of our beings. We bonded in a way that as far as I knew was unbreakable. Bonded, and we barely knew each other.

"This was clearly a mutual thing." V's voice wasn't quite as calm anymore either. They pointed at their own collarbone and the jagged ring of teeth marks dipping down toward their breast. I took one look and wanted to rush forward and take that damnable tit into my mouth and start sucking like it was fucking ambrosia. I shook my head, holding myself back from doing anything stupid.

This wasn't me. I didn't fall for anyone, never mind this damned quickly. This was my time to connect with my wolf and get closure from my mother. This was not the time to go and bind myself to some random wolf whose life I'd surely fucked up no end.

And yet, there was this part of me that craved their touch, craved to touch them. Like there was something inside me being drawn to V. Was that my wolf? Was it the mate bond, or something else entirely? I wanted to understand more of what was going on, but the anger running through me made sitting still and waiting for an explanation impossible.

"You said we'd take it as slow as I needed to," I said, shaking my head as I backed away from them.

"Yes, and I also pointed out that this is a mutual thing. You gave as good as you got."

"I don't remember that!"

"How can you not? You and your wolf worked together to do this."

"I told you before, I can't control what my wolf does. She doesn't talk to me. She doesn't want anything to do with me!"

They snorted. "Bullshit. Anyone your age can control their wolf by now. It's not like it's hard."

"Well, thanks for that obvious tip, but I can't, all right? I can't shift at will! I have no control over this monster inside me, that's why I was so afraid last night!"

They raised their hands in a placating gesture. "Look, let's get dressed and get out of here, then we can talk about this, okay? My place isn't far from here. We can go there and figure out where to go next."

"No! I'm not going anywhere with you." As if to prove that point, I spun on my heel and started walking into the trees. "I'm done with all this. I need a pair of shoes and I'm going to finish what I came here to do."

"Heather, wait—"

I didn't. I didn't wait. I didn't wait to hear what else they were going to say, what else they had to tell me. I didn't want to hear it. Just another way that I was broken, different than everyone else. I wasn't in control of my wolf. I couldn't make her listen to me, I couldn't wrest control from her when she was free. Whatever my wolf did last night was not with my permission. I didn't want this, not like this. If ever I wanted this to happen, I wanted to be a part of it, to have some kind of control over it. Instead that had been taken from me by my own wolf.

I needed to get back to my car and change, then figure out what I was going to do about my mother and Summer. Figure out a way to fix how my wolf felt about me, about this whole doing things without my knowledge thing. I was not here to get werewolf-hitched.

I stomped off into the woods, working on finding my way out to the nearest pathway or roadway or something that denoted civilization. I was sure V would be quick to try and get on my trail. I started running faster, not slowing when I came to a walking path that wound through the trees until it hit a roadway that had a big sign proclaiming Mill Creek Ravine. I knew where I was now—perks of growing up in the city before I ran away.

I slowed down and tried to look like a normal person walking along the sidewalk early in the morning—despite my lack of shoes and clothes in general. I ran a hand through my hair and grimaced when my fingers caught in the tangles and pulled. Several leaves fell to the ground too. I knew I looked pretty terrible. Probably like I woke up after a night of wild sex in the ravine, if nothing else. I couldn't help but laugh a little. I felt I was in the same place I was a year ago, all but living on the streets while being treated like shit by the rest of my pack.

But I was in a better pack now. Wren and Natalie cared

about me, helped me as much as they could. Wren was the kind of pack leader I wanted to have. But she wasn't here right now because I had decided that I could handle this on my own. That I could take on my family, and the greatest abuser of my short life, all by my lonesome. How stupid— No. No, I had to stop that. These self-deprecating spirals I fell into were getting harder and harder to break out of the farther I was from my support system.

I patted at my pockets. Say one thing for the sundress being too big, at least it had pockets. My car keys were still there, which meant I had a mode of transportation—if I found my car. My cards were with my phone in the other pocket, meaning I had money too. With a long sigh I headed west back toward the hospital, stopping in at a small store where I picked up a pair of flip-flops for my feet and a sandwich and drink. I called a cab, sat outside the store with my breakfast, and tried my best not to pine for the werewolf I had left behind, despite how strong the pull was.

I closed my eyes and let out a long breath. I might be connected to V now, but I didn't need to take direction from them. It was clear their pack considered them a dominant, but that didn't mean I needed to be their submissive. I was my own person. My goal was to become whole for the first time since I could remember. I wasn't about to let them take that away from me.

CHAPTER SEVEN

V

I started after Heather before looking down at myself and realizing I was still naked. As much as our little clearing was effectively hidden in the trees, I knew the walking path was nearby. It was too busy a path for me to go parading out without clothes. I didn't need the police being called on me.

Besides, Heather needed some time, that was clear. It wasn't like I forced the mate bond on her. Last night when I took back control of my wolf she seemed into it. She wanted it. We had spent an hour kissing and touching and nipping at each other before we finished with the mate bite.

She was into it.

I slammed a fist into a tree with a thunderous crack, and a bolt of pain shot through me. It woke me up better than any cup of coffee.

Heather had been into it. Yes, she wanted to take it slow. I could remember clearly what she'd said in the dreamscape we shared. But after that she was completely into it. I mean, I had the marks to show for it. What the hell had happened between then and now that changed her mind? Or did she change it? Was it something to do with her wolf? She kept saying she had no control over the beast inside of her. The monster, she said. She called herself a monster. I certainly didn't see her that way. Who in her life did? Her Alpha? An Alpha who treats their wolves like they're monsters is building a pack that acts like monsters. If it was her Alpha, well, I was going to have to meet this person and have a long conversation with them. I wasn't afraid of standing up to an Alpha.

"Yeah," I said under my breath, "unless it's your own father."

I pushed the thoughts out of my mind and got dressed, pulling on my jeans, tank top, and leather jacket. Not exactly walking or jogging clothes, but it would keep me from getting pulled aside by the cops while I made the short walk home.

My apartment wasn't far from the ravine—a location I chose on purpose, not exactly for nights like last night, but for similar occasions. This meant I could spend the nights I needed to shift in the trees, where few people would be in the middle of the night for fear of coyotes and possible muggers. I knew the pathways, knew the lights to avoid, and worked hard to make sure no one thought to call animal control about a wild wolf in the ravine.

I let myself into the small apartment and tossed the jacket on the coatrack by the door. It wasn't a large place, one bedroom with a tiny bathroom and a galley kitchen with barely enough room for a small two-seater kitchen table. The living room was the largest area, with a couch, television, and my game systems set up for downtime fun.

I went to the fridge and stood there with the door open for a good few minutes. My thoughts drifted back to the russet-furred wolf and the beautiful woman who claimed to have no control. It made sense if she was maybe in her teens, just through her first few shifts and learning to communicate with her wolf. But Heather was closer to my age. By this time, unless something really hinky was going on, she should be at one with her wolf. Hell, that's when a wolf finds out if they're an Alpha or not. I didn't smell that kind of power in her, but she was still a full-grown wolf. I let the fridge close and rested my forehead against it.

Was she using her wolf as a scapegoat? Claiming that she couldn't control her wolf when the beast did something that she didn't like? She didn't seem the type, though. There was something else up with her, something I didn't know. Whatever I had interrupted at the hospital was only another piece of the puzzle that was my new mate.

I rubbed a hand along my collarbone, feeling the small bumps of the scabs from the mate bite. It would heal in another day, two at most. It would scar. The bite was meant to scar. It was a permanent sign, a reminder that we were bonded to the most important person in our lives. Our mate. More important than the dominants in the pack. More important than the Alpha. Our fated mates were special, incredibly rare, and a gift from the Mother of Wolves that I wasn't sure I deserved.

And now, because of Heather, I was going to have to go to war with the rest of my pack.

Tomorrow night, my father planned to announce my mating to Sinclair. But that was no longer an option for me. Like I'd said last night, my fated mate landed in my lap at the perfect time. But that didn't mean I didn't have to find a way to try and explain it to the pack, explain it to my Alpha and my mother and everyone else. Everyone who thought that I needed to do things their way. Everyone who wanted me to be different than I was.

Did Heather want me to be a particular type of person? I didn't exactly get to spend a lot of time with her. From her shift last night to the fight this morning, there wasn't a lot of conversation that couldn't be thought of as a dream. And damn, that was an interesting dream. I'd never met someone who had their fated mate before, so I wondered if that weird dream thing was normal between Heather and me. And if it was usually full of that much conversation.

I groaned and turned away from the fridge. I wasn't a saint. I'd never profess to being one. I wanted Heather in a way that felt absolutely primal. Being with her wolf last night, especially after I shifted myself, was one of the best nights of my life. She was fun, playful, and enjoyable. And tough too. She wouldn't lie down and let me win when we were wrestling, either. She was a breath of fresh air in a stagnant world. I needed her. And luckily, I had a good idea of where to find her.

A knock on the door shocked me from my thoughts. I considered pretending not to be home, but the timidness of the knock made me think I knew who was there. I sighed and tried to ignore my hunger pangs as I headed for the door.

"Hi, Mom."

She stood on the other side of the door, her eyes dark and worried.

"Are you all right? You didn't check in last night." She pushed her way past me and into the apartment. I stood by and let her pass.

"By all means, come in."

"Don't you be flippant with me. I came here because I was worried about what you were going to do last night."

"Why? Because you decided to let my father dictate who I am allowed to be with for the rest of my life?" I moved past her, heading back into the kitchen.

"Val, it's not like that."

"Bullshit it's not! Forcing me to mate with someone? Really? And you thought I wouldn't be pissed off about it?"

"I knew you'd be angry, but you need to look at it from his point of view. We need a strong pairing with you and another wolf. You need to give him an Alpha so we can keep the family line going. Sinclair is—"

"A self-righteous bully who thinks that he can do whatever the hell he wants," I yelled. "And you expect me to just start trying to pop out pups as soon as he can have his way with me? After everything I've told you, explained to you who I am, what I like?" I stared her down. "How could you?"

"I told you to let me talk him down. I can try and make sure it's not Sinclair. Maybe it could be one of the other dominants. But we need you to have children. You are our only child, and I'm getting past that age. I'm almost a century old, Val. I can't give him the heir he wants. Now it's up to you."

"Fuck you." I shook my head. "You don't give a shit at all about me and what I want." I slammed a hand down on my kitchen table. "All you care about is what you and Dad want."

"No, we care about the pack and the future of it. Like it or not, you're part of that—" She cut herself off when her eyes caught on my shoulder. "What is that?"

"What's what?"

"What is on your shoulder?"

I flinched and turned my side away from her view in a brief moment of embarrassment. But I had no reason to be embarrassed. I was proud of being mated. At least, I should be. Maybe if things had gone better with Heather this morning I could say I was.

"What does it look like?"

My mother snarled at me. Like literally snarled, as if her wolf was close to the surface. "It looks like you went out and got the first stupid wolf you could find to mate with you! Do you have any idea what you've done?"

"I know exactly what I did! I found my true mate and I did what we both wanted." I was not about to tell her about the little misunderstanding this morning. That was between me and my mate.

Her eyes widened in shock. "Your true mate? Are you sure?"

"I'm positive. As soon as I caught her scent last night I knew who she was to me. My wolf wouldn't let me forget it."

I waited for another tongue-lashing. Maybe a few *if your father finds outs* and a *for the good of the pack.* Instead a smile lit up her face like I hadn't seen in a long time.

"You're not lying to me, are you?" she said. Her voice sounded breathy, like she could barely believe it. "You really met your true mate. That's amazing. That's…incredible."

"You…you're not angry about it?"

She let out a long breath, and it looked like the tension that had kept her rigid finally drained away. She took a seat at the table and I sat across from her.

"I should be. I am. But I'm also not. It's different, you know?"

I shook my head. "I don't understand. You were just tearing into me for not putting the pack first, and now you're happy about it?"

"I didn't say I was happy about it. But true mates are a gift from the Mother of Wolves. We never know when, or if, we'll ever find them. And you know that if we're already mated, then that's it. We don't get to have our true mate. I'm…I'm exceptionally happy for you that you found your true mate, I truly am. Is it going to cause a lot of problems within the pack? Definitely. But that is something we will have to figure out. I would never ask anyone to give up the chance to have their true mate, for anything."

In some ways it was like seeing my mother in a new light, and at the same time being reunited with a part of her that

I hadn't seen in years. Like time spent enforcing the will of the Alpha in our pack had drained her of her smile, of her happiness. She looked truly happy for me. And I missed that feeling.

"Thank you, Mom."

She clapped her hands, smiling wider than I'd seen in a very long time. "So, where is she? I want to meet her."

"How did you know she's a she?"

She looked at me like I was stupid. "Because I do know my child, V. The Mother wouldn't have given you a gift that it would break you to have."

I grunted my acknowledgment but wasn't sure what else to say to that. The fact that she knew it would break me to be mated to Sinclair or someone else like him, and that she wanted me to go through with it not two minutes ago, was still at the forefront of my mind.

"She's not here."

"Well, I can see that." She sniffed the air with almost a curious expression. "I don't smell her here at all. Did you not spend the night together?"

"I took her out for a run last night. We ended up in the ravine."

"I hope you treated her right."

"I'm not an asshole, Mother. I did what I could to make her comfortable." I hesitated. I really didn't want to tell her about Heather's blow-up this morning, but there was something I needed to know. "Mom, do you know if our wolves can carry out the mate bite without us knowing?"

She tapped her fingers on the table, taking long moments before finally responding. "I suppose there is a chance of it happening. I've never heard of it, personally, but it could happen."

"What about someone not being in communication with

their wolf? Like they have no idea what the wolf side of them does, and vice versa."

"That happens a lot with young wolves. When you were a teenager first learning about your wolf, you didn't know or remember what your wolf did. Why are you asking these questions?"

I shook my head again. "Nothing. No reason. I'm...trying to figure out something."

"Is there something wrong with her or her wolf?"

"No," I answered a little too quickly, "no, she doesn't seem to be in great contact with her wolf. But she's not a teen going through her first shifts either. It's odd. Like her growth was...stunted or something."

"Well, this is a conversation you should be having with her."

"I plan to, I do."

She gave me a wicked smile. "That's why she's not here this morning, isn't it? She got scared of the mate bite?"

Damn. My mother was too smart for her own good. "I tried to talk her down, but she only got angrier."

She stood up and came around the table, wrapping her arms around me in an odd kind of hug. She hadn't tried to hold me like this in a very long time. "Either way, I'm proud of you for finding your mate. You will make it work with her. I know you will."

Despite the awkwardness of the hug, I still melted into it a little, laying my head on her arm. "Are you going to tell Father?"

She let out a long breath. "I don't know yet."

"Don't tell him?" I asked softly. "Let me do it, please. I don't want him mad at you."

"It is not only him you'll have to worry about. Half the pack already knows you are promised to Sinclair."

"What? He said he was announcing it tomorrow night."

"Yeah, but you know Sinclair. He couldn't keep his mouth shut. Everyone's expecting it now."

I snarled under my breath, and her arms abruptly disappeared from around me.

"I hate that man."

"Well, keep an eye on him. He isn't used to not getting his way. He and your father are going to be furious about this." Her finger found the raised bite marks. "But for what it's worth, I'm happy for you."

"Thanks, Mom. I appreciate it."

She patted me on the shoulder. "Good luck."

I watched her let herself out, then leaned back in my chair, letting out a long sigh of relief. One parental figure down. Now I had to deal with the other one. Somehow, I knew the other one wasn't going to go nearly as well.

Chapter Eight

Heather

The closer the cab got to the hospital, the more I was regretting ever coming back here. I'd thought I put it all behind me the day I ran away, and again the day that Wren freed my wolf. I didn't need my mother's approval for who I was. I didn't need my family to understand for the first time ever that I felt like a whole person—more or less.

I thought I was whole, but it seemed my wolf had other ideas. She wasn't willing to work with me. She'd made that abundantly clear last night. Could wolves mate without their human sides realizing it? Was that even a thing? I mean, it had obviously happened, but was there a part of me that was along for the ride, a part of me saying *Yup, getting bonded to a stranger for the rest of my long life sounds like a fucking fantastic idea, sign me up.*

I groaned and shook my head, ignoring the look I got from the driver as he pulled into the parking lot. I silently made sure he got paid and then got out, waiting for him to leave, or at least move the fucking car before I headed out into the lot to find the sedan.

Then I caught a whiff of V, and I swear my mouth began to water. What the hell was this now? I couldn't go back to my car without something there to remind me of them? And what the hell was their scent doing all over the sedan? Wren was going to kill me if it still smelled of them when I got back. Would their scent come off in a car wash? Or was it like metaphysical or something and would stick around forever?

While my mind raced with possibilities and what-ifs regarding everything that wasn't truly important in my life, my body decided to start running on autopilot. A moment passed as I cleared my head and found myself standing not in front of the sedan anymore, but instead staring at a fun-looking motorcycle parked a few spots away. The scent of V was stronger here, and I could feel an odd rumbling of approval in my chest that was not something I felt entirely in control of.

I pressed a hand against my chest, the other against my mouth. Was this my wolf? Was I feeling what she was feeling, what she was thinking? I knew enough to know that there would never truly be words between us, but feelings and emotions could be interpreted. That's how it was supposed to work, anyway. Whatever this meant, it made one thing abundantly clear: My wolf wanted V, no matter how bad the idea might truthfully be. This wasn't a fairy tale, after all.

Like a door being shut in my face, the rumbling in my chest suddenly cut off, leaving me feeling empty once more. I fought back the tears that threatened to fall and shook my head.

I wondered what Wren would have said in the moment, wondered if she would know how to bring the wolf out more instead of keeping that door shut between us. Then my traitorous mind turned to V and what they might say about it. How would they feel knowing that their mate was so completely broken?

"Damn it," I muttered and pulled myself away from those thoughts as well as the bike, heading back to the car. I grabbed some clothes from my bag and slid into the back seat, ignoring all possibility of being ashamed to be seen changing in the car. I slipped into a pair of jeans and a sports bra with a loose tank over top. I pulled my hair back into a ponytail, then pulled it out again, then put it up again. It was at this point that I realized I was putting off what I really needed to do. What I fucking came here to do. To talk to my mother, get my closure for her making me feel like a monster for most of my life, and to tell her that for the first time in forever I felt like a whole person.

Even if it was a lie.

Fuck!

I slammed a fist against the seat, then again, and again. My wrist twisted after the third hit and I yelped, cradling the hurt appendage to me as the tears slid down. Fuck her. Fuck all of this bullshit. Fuck V and fuck Summer and fuck my damned mother and fuck my damned wolf!

Was closure such a big deal? I mean, I could leave. Head back to Terabend, tell Wren that I did what I needed to do and came home. No need to tell her about my mate. Or my sister or mom. No need to say that I chickened out and didn't do what I came here to do.

Damn it.

I got out of the car, making sure I kept my phone and the keys on me, and headed for the front doors again. I didn't bother with the front desk, simply made a beeline to the elevators and headed up toward my mother's room.

The scent of the hospital was worse than it had been last night. Or maybe that was my wolf's way of saying she didn't like the scent, but either way it was definitely something on my mind as I slipped into the quiet room and closed the door most of the way behind me. It was like walking through a curtain of silence, the only sounds in the room being the soft beeping of the machines. Of course my mother was in a room by herself. She would expect nothing less, and Summer was probably quick to make sure it happened.

Speaking of Summer, where the hell was she? Had she already been by this morning or did I scare her so badly that she didn't want to risk meeting me here again? Or maybe she thought I'd ripped our mother to shreds when I couldn't control my wolf last night.

If it wasn't for V, I very well might've.

I let out a sigh. I still couldn't stop thinking of V. Was this going to be a constant now? As much as I hoped not, I honestly felt like I didn't mind the idea either. There were worse people to be obsessed with.

I grabbed the chair sitting nearby and pulled it up to the bed. I sat with my back to the door, hands on the bed, equal parts hoping and dreading having her wake up while I was there. I wanted to talk to her, to understand why she did what she did to me. But at the same time, what if it only made things worse? What if all it did was make the truth harder to bear? I was a monster, after all. I didn't know if I could control myself and not hurt her depending on what she might say.

I was scared. Plain and simple. I sat in that damned chair and listened to the machines beep, and looked down at my mother looking so frail with the sterile hospital scents in the air, and I felt barely anything more than fear.

Fear. I lived in fear. Of myself, of my family. Of life.

"And it's all your fault," I said to her prone form. "You made me feel like I didn't belong, like I would never belong. Like it didn't matter what I thought or felt. Do you know how many years I thought there was something wrong with me because of you? Because you made me feel that way? And now, now that I'm supposed to be whole, I'm really not. I'm still broken, shattered into so many pieces that I don't think I'll ever get put back together again."

I laid my head in my hands, hoping against everything that maybe I'd get an answer, and dreading the idea all at the same time. Would she listen? Would she apologize, tell me she was wrong and ask forgiveness? I shook my head. Not likely. There was a better chance of the moon falling from the sky than for Cecily McKenna to ever admit to any sort of wrongdoing. Especially if what she'd done was *for the best.*

I opened my mouth to say more when the door behind me opened and a nurse walked in. We glanced at each other, and it was like she could read all the emotions on my face, giving me a look that was equal parts weary and apologetic. She moved into the room with a grace I wished I could mimic and didn't say a thing as she went through whatever procedures she needed to. I didn't distract her from her work.

Then she was gone and I was alone with my mother once more.

"I'm broken," I said again, "and I don't know how to put myself back together. I thought having my wolf, being free, would fix things. But it didn't. And all of this because, what, you thought it would punish my father? That cursing me and trapping my wolf inside me would somehow hurt him? You didn't think of me at all, did you?"

I paused like I was waiting for an answer, but it was not to come. Would I ever get a straight answer from her? Maybe, if she lived.

Goddess, I didn't even know what was wrong with her. And it might make me a terrible daughter, but I didn't think I wanted to know.

Even when I wasn't a wolf, I was still a monster. I was a terrible person. Blaming everything on her, when I was as much to blame, wasn't I? I was the one living this half-life. Being a burden on those around me. I was useless to a pack, at first because I couldn't shift, and now because my wolf wouldn't cooperate. I put pressure on Wren and Natalie, who deserved time to be together instead of dealing with someone like me.

And now I had become attached to someone like V, who didn't deserve to be stuck with a useless, wolf-less mistake like me.

I laid my head down on my arms, letting the tears run down and soak into the blanket covering her. Why was I wasting my tears on my mother? I didn't want to cry over the person who destroyed my ability to trust what I felt. She didn't deserve my tears. Instead, I cried for the little girl I was, the one that didn't get a chance to grow up to be a normal werewolf.

I choked back a chuckle. *Normal werewolf.* As if there were such a thing.

I lifted my head as a new scent drifted into the room. I sniffled, taking in a deeper breath, and immediately felt calmer. What the hell was V doing here?

I shook my head. It didn't matter anymore. They were going to find out who I really was at some point and realize what a mistake they'd made last night in giving me the mate bite.

"Are you here to make sure I don't tear her apart?" I asked, raising my voice enough to make sure they heard me. "Not that she wouldn't deserve it."

There was a soft chuckle behind me.

"If you did, it would make things a lot more difficult for me."

"Yeah? Why's that?"

"Because I would be the only thing standing between my mate and the rest of my pack."

I snorted. "And I know which side you'd come down on. I'm not stupid."

I flinched when a hand settled softly on my shoulder. "I think you have no idea who I am or what I would do."

"Maybe, but I also know how things work. No one likes a rogue wolf in their territory. You have no reason to interfere with whatever they want to do."

"You're my mate. I wouldn't let them hurt you."

I scoffed. "Bullshit."

"You talk a lot about things you don't know or don't understand."

"Because I know how the world works. I'm a monster, a freak, a burden to everyone around me. And monsters don't get happy endings."

The entire time I had refused to look at them, but then a hand touched my chin, pulled my head up, and brought me face-to-face with my mate. I stared into those hard, hazel eyes and watched them soften.

"You are not a monster. Whoever has told you this lied to you."

My eyes flicked toward the unmoving body of my mother before I managed to close them and pull away from those soft fingers.

"I know what I am," I murmured.

I heard V sigh beside me.

"I think we need to talk."

"You're not going to take me to your pack for judgment? For running around their territory without permission? Mating with one of their dominants without the Alpha's blessing? I know that's a big deal."

They shook their head, some of their hair falling over the undercut on the right side. Whatever it was inside me that pulled me toward this person was as strong as it had been last night, and I desperately wanted to run my hands through that hair.

"Heather, I'm not going to let them do anything to you. You're my mate, and we're going to figure out what's going on. I want to know why you're here. I want to know everything about you."

"It's a long story." V might not realize it, but this wasn't a warning to take lightly.

"Then let me take you for breakfast—" They cut themselves off as they checked their watch. "Lunch. To a late lunch. Then we can talk all we want."

I stared at V for a long moment, taking in the fresh jeans and tank top they were wearing under that same leather jacket that looked like it was damned well painted on them. It was such a good look for them and it worked so damned well, and I wanted to peel them out of their clothes piece by piece by piece—

Stop it!

Whatever the hell was inside me needed to stop that shit if I was ever going to be able to think clearly about this person. I was not ready to go into heat with my mate. I was not ready to throw myself at them. We needed to take it slow.

Going for lunch would be taking it slow.

"Okay," I finally agreed. I stood up from the chair without offering my mother the smallest of parting glances. "Let's go."

Chapter Nine

Heather

I climbed off the motorcycle, still feeling my legs vibrating from the ride, and stared at the glowing neon sign sitting over what looked like a freaking hole-in-the-wall bar. Like, I knew dingy bars and diners—I'd eaten in enough of them—but this was nothing but a door and the sign. And yet it seemed strikingly familiar.

"I thought we were going for lunch?" I asked.

V smiled. "We are. Here."

I stared at the sign for a moment longer. "Ripley's Steakhouse?"

"Best steak in the city, especially for us."

I turned my attention to them. "You mean…"

"Owned and operated by Ripley, a member of the Raines pack."

I took an involuntary step back. "Is this a good idea? I mean, your pack isn't going to be happy with me, will they?"

"Why not? They don't know you're in town."

"But your wolf at the hospital—"

"Told me about you. It's my job to deal with possible rogue wolves and other dangerous shifters. I've decided you're not dangerous, so no one has anything to worry about."

I bristled. "Of course I'm dangerous. I can't control my wolf—"

They held a hand up to stop me. "I know. I understand. But if you're feeling the same things that I am, I know that my being close to you is enough to calm your wolf. I figure staying near you will be enough to keep her in check until we can figure something else out. And this way I can make sure you don't lose control on some innocent old lady."

The last was said with a smile, but the words hit me like a hammer slamming into my heart.

A second later their smile fell when they realized what they'd said. "Heather, I'm sorry, I didn't mean it like—"

I shook my head. "It's fine. Let's go in and eat, okay? Then you can tell me what the hell is going on between us, because I sure as hell don't get it."

"That's why we're here. No matter what happens, Ripley doesn't allow violence in her establishment. Not even from her own pack. We'll be able to talk safely here."

There was still something nagging in the back of my head about this place, but I followed V through the front door and into a dim world of cooked meat and soft country music. Tables took up most of the space, small ones that would have trouble seating four people with their meals. Along one wall was a set of larger booths that looked like they rarely saw use, and adjacent to that was a long bar with doors that led to the back area. The lighting was very dim, like walking out at midnight with nothing but the full moon for your guide. The entire room smelled of meat, cooked and not cooked, and it woke something inside me, like that door that my wolf liked to keep closed between the two of us opened barely a crack. Suddenly I could smell the underlying scents of the room, sweat and booze, and underneath everything else the faintest tinge of metallic blood.

And with those scents came a fleeting memory that I struggled to hold on to. Images of the bar, a little brighter, with more people and less dingy. A warm hand in mine, engulfing mine…a smile directed at me, flashing white teeth that looked sharper than they should've. The eyes that looked down at me were not my mother's. No, it was someone else.

I blinked and the recollection was over. I was back in the restaurant, my hand being tugged by V as they looked at me, confused.

"Are you okay?"

I shook my head. "I've been here before."

"What?"

"I've been in here before, I think. When I was a child."

Their eyes narrowed. "Let's find a seat, then we can talk about it, all right?"

I let them lead me toward a table on the far side of the room. It was the same size as all the rest but was tucked into the corner with only two chairs at it. They pulled out a chair for me, all cordial-like, and I sat as they took the chair against the wall. Their eyes weren't on me but on the rest of the room, particularly the front door. It made me wonder how true their earlier words had been, about putting themselves between me and the rest of their pack. Because right now I was feeling pretty pinned between the two.

I took a glance around, noting a few other tables occupied by quiet individuals, but none of them seemed interested in newcomers. Save for one group my eyes landed on in the largest booth on the far wall. They seemed interested in V and me, quickly looking away as my eyes drifted over them. I turned to see if V had noticed the exchange and found their attention solely on me.

"Don't worry about them," V said as if they knew exactly what I was worried about. "They won't bring you any harm."

"That's easier said than done," I replied, a little more flippant than I probably should've been. "I'm trapped in a den of wolves here. And as far as I know only one of them likes me."

They cracked a smile. "That's one more than none. And any of them that don't want to make me an enemy would be wise to leave you alone."

I snorted. "Is that how it works in your pack? Are you the Alpha all of a sudden?"

"No, but I am his child, which gives me some sway in things. I'm also his Knight and considered a dominant, so that prevents most of the other wolves in the pack standing against me unless they want an ass kicking."

I pretended that I wasn't idly considering getting into a fight just to see V step in and finish it for me. That image was generating a heat in my core that wasn't completely coming from the animal side of me.

I cleared my throat, pushing those thoughts away for a moment. "So your pack is still into the dominant-submissive thing."

A dark look crossed their face. "As far as I know, every pack is. I think it's fucking stupid and we need to get with the times, but I'm not an Alpha."

"I've seen how submissives get treated. Hell, I lived it."

"I could tell. Your trust in me as a dominant wolf is certainly tentative. I'm assuming you've had a bad experience, like most of us did."

"Fuck yeah I did. It was made worse because I—" I cut myself off. We had agreed to talk, but was I ready to empty my heart and mind to this person? Would they understand what I went through, or tell me to get the hell over it? "But that's over now. I have a pack that doesn't believe in that shit. We might only be few, but it works for us. And I don't—didn't—have to worry about being mated to some random dominant just for the hell of it."

"That's something no wolf should have to worry about. We should be free to seek out our true mates—or at least consider mating for love. Not to control the number of wolves in the pack and make sure the dominants are happy so they don't cause trouble."

"I've seen the fallout firsthand," I said. I thought about Wren's story and my own part in it.

I was about to say more when a matronly woman walked up to the table with two bottles of beer, placing them silently between us. V caught her eye and smiled, but there was no change of expression on the woman's sour-looking face.

"Heather, this is Ripley. It's her place. Ripley, this is—"

Ripley shook her head. "I don't want to know, kid." Her voice was a low growl that sounded only half human. "I don't get mixed up in pack politics."

V's eyes darkened. "You know, then."

"Word got around."

I looked back and forth between them. "What? Word about what?"

"Shit," V said, "I thought I'd have more time."

"More time for what?"

Ripley shook her head. "I don't allow fighting in here, you know that."

"That's half the reason we're here," V said, "I needed somewhere at least a little safe."

I opened my mouth to ask what they were talking about, but Ripley gave me a look that killed the words in my throat. She looked from me to V and back again.

"Congratulations, for what it's worth." She walked away as I turned to V.

"What the hell was that?"

"Ripley. She's always been a little odd, but she's good people."

I held my head in my hands. "Ugh! I just feel like there's so much going on that I don't understand!"

V tugged one of my hands away and held it clasped in both of theirs. "And that's my fault as much as anything. I'm sorry it's been such a whirlwind of a day and there's so much going on. This wasn't a great time for all of this, but it happens when it happens, I guess. I'm sorry, Heather."

I shook my head. "It's okay, it is, only I feel so overwhelmed. With everything going on with my mom, and now this? I never meant to cause so much trouble."

"It's not your fault. You're not the cause of the trouble, believe me."

"It's hard to believe you when that's certainly the way it seems."

"You have a habit of blaming yourself for things you cannot control."

I snorted loudly. "Everyone else has been doing it, figured I'd jump on the bandwagon." I tugged my hand back as I winced. That sounded a little too *woe is me* even for my taste and I quickly added, "I mean, I've had a shitty run of things."

They let my hand go without argument. "I was going to say that something must've happened. Is this to do with your mom? Is she the woman at the hospital?"

I nodded and told them about the call from Summer that started everything the night before. Was it really only last night that this had all started? It felt like so much had happened since then. I took a quick sip of the beer in front of me, then a longer drink. Damn. That was surprisingly good.

"Ripley's microbrew," V said, as if reading my mind.

"It's good."

"She'll be happy to know that." They took a sip of their

own brew, closing their eyes as if to savor it for a moment before focusing on me again.

"Forgive me for saying so, but what the hell was your Alpha thinking letting you come here all alone? This close to the full moon and without letting the local Alpha know what was going on?" They shook their head.

I sighed. "That was my fault. On all counts. I told Wren I would be fine, that I could handle it. She didn't believe me, but she had enough on her hands with her own mate, she didn't need to be looking after me too." I took another sip of beer and enjoyed the slight burn in my throat. "And I did plan to see the Alpha, it was my next stop after the hospital. And, well, you saw how that turned out."

"You lost control, I came in, and thus started our journey together."

"You make it sound so poetic."

They grinned. "It's a gift." They took another drink. "I know I'm going to be asking a lot of questions, but I need to know more about what's happening. I need to know why you thought it was so important to come here when you knew that there was a chance you couldn't control your wolf."

"I know, I know. It's not exactly easy to talk about."

"Is this something to do with you not being able to communicate with her?"

"It includes that, yes," I admitted, rubbing a hand up and down my leg anxiously. Damn it. How many times in my life was I going to have to tell this fucking story? "I just...there's a good reason why I can't control my wolf, why she doesn't talk to me."

"You make it sound like her fault. Like she chooses not to."

"No. No, it's entirely my own fault. Because I was born the way I was."

Their eyes narrowed. "What do you mean by that?"

"Because I'm a werewolf. Because I was cursed. Because I don't know how to make my wolf understand that I didn't want it to happen, that I—"

V slammed their bottle on the table hard enough to jostle mine and silence the rest of the dingy bar. I pushed my chair back a little but stayed seated, knowing that the predator inside the person across from me had to be close to the surface.

"Cursed? You think being a werewolf is a curse?"

I shook my head again and again. "No—no! That's not what I meant at all. I swear it."

A hand on my cheek halted my head and I looked up to see V leaning deep over the table, one eye the normal hazel that I kept looking deeply into. The other had started to lighten and change, showing me that golden hue of the eyes of their wolf.

"I'm sorry," I whispered.

V was quiet for a long moment, unmoving as the warmth of their palm radiated into my cheek and I fought the urge to nuzzle against it.

"It's my fault," I murmured. "It's always my fault. All of it."

"Tell me what happened." Their voice was as soft as mine and their hand lingered on my cheek before the fingers slid down toward my chin and they sat back in their chair. That tiny opening in the doorway between myself and my wolf creaked open a little further as if my beast wanted them to keep touching us, to not move away. I had to agree with her.

I finished off the rest of my beer and took a deep breath. Then I started at the beginning.

"I'm sorry. You'd think I could start this without issue, the number of times I've had to tell it," I said with a soft sigh. "I was born here in Edmonton. My dad was a werewolf, my mom a human. She didn't find out about him until after she was pregnant. From what I can tell, she didn't handle it well."

"It would probably be quite jarring," V said.

"I don't remember him at all. At least I didn't until..." I drifted off, remembering the odd sort of memory that hit me at the entrance to the steakhouse. My wolf's memory. Not mine. I was certain of that now. It meant my father was in my life at least once when I was a child. I shook my head and continued. "My mother hired a witch to curse me when I was a kid. She knew I'd be a wolf like my dad, and the witch locked my wolf in a cage so I could never shift."

V stared at me with wide eyes. I reached over the table and stole their bottle of microbrew, mine already empty.

"When I found out about it, I confronted her. She said it was for my own good. So I could be normal. She didn't understand what it was like to be living half a life like that. I ran away, went east and ended up with a pack called the Cardinals, in Winnipeg. They took me in and promised to help, but the Alpha couldn't be bothered to deal with someone he labeled a submissive. I was treated lower than that because I couldn't shift. I was barely north of nothing to them."

I took a sip of the stolen drink, giving V a chance to say something. Instead they stayed quiet, pensive almost, like they were focused on committing my story to memory.

"Then an opportunity arose to get help. A wolf wanted to attack another territory, to destabilize it, if not attack the Alpha directly. He promised to help me if I helped him, so I went along with it. But...well, he failed. And I stayed. I joined that Alpha's pack, worked to gain her trust and repay her for her kindness." And I knew that I would never truly be able to repay Wren for all of her kindness. For all that she had done for me. "Wren and her mate, Natalie, helped me break my curse with assistance from Rias, a local witch."

"That's amazing," V commented, hanging on to my every word.

"It was amazing. I was free. For the first time in my life, I was free." And in some ways it still felt like that. "But it didn't last long."

"What do you mean?"

"I mean that my wolf acts like she's still locked up. Except for the full moon, I can't shift. I can't talk to her, communicate at all. She's closed the door between us and I don't know how to break through."

My voice drifted off softly as I tried to ignore the tears that had started rolling down my cheeks. As many times as I'd thought about it, talked about it, it always came to the same result. I cried for what I couldn't have. The time I couldn't reclaim. I sat there and waited for my mate to say something, to tell me that I was too broken for them, to say that I would be nothing but a burden.

I held my breath and waited.

CHAPTER TEN

V

Listening to Heather's story, I could barely contain my wolf's urge to pick up the table between us and throw it across the room. Not that I could blame the beast inside me. If I wasn't worried about getting on Ripley's bad side, I might've let it happen anyway.

Who the hell would do something like that? And to a child? Heather called herself a monster, but it was only because other people had done monstrous things to her and made her think it was her own damned fault. She apologized again and again, accepting the blame—the fault—for everything that happened to her as something that she deserved.

It was all such terrible, abusive bullshit. She had to be so damned strong to still be going. To live like she had for so long. I saw her in a new light now, her story clearing up so many of the questions I'd had about her. Not all of them, but enough that I knew I had someone who was truly special.

And she was my mate.

My mate.

And woe to anyone who messed with my fucking mate.

"So why come back so quickly?" I asked finally, after

she had finished not only her story but my bottle of Ripley's microbrew. "I mean, you don't owe your family anything. You could have waited the three nights of the full moon before showing up."

She let out a heavy sigh. "I don't know, honestly. I guess for the same reason I never changed my phone number. I wanted them to want me back. To need me. I wanted to know that they still thought of me. I never considered that I'd get a call one night telling me my mom was in the hospital. After that, it was like…like moving on autopilot."

"So what happened at the hospital to make you lose control?"

"Just—just being there. Being in that room with the sounds and the smells and my mother in the bed. My sister was acting like nothing had gone wrong between us and she was happy to see me. Like, really happy. For the first time I started to feel like maybe they knew they were wrong and they wanted some sort of relationship with me!"

"And it all went wrong?"

She laughed and took another drink of her third microbrew—Ripley reappearing time and again with new bottles like a specter.

"I should've known better. Summer thought I had gone away to find a…a cure for what I am. So I could be like them. She thought I'd succeeded when I walked into the hospital room. I never thought she would ever greet me like a sister after the fight we had so many years ago. But she hugged me. Told me she missed me." She shook her head. "Between all of that and my mom in the bed, it riled me up so much my wolf decided she would take charge. It was all I could do to stop myself. And of course Summer made it worse by freaking out and calling me a monster."

"You're not a monster." She had this bad habit of doing

that, of making herself out to be the bad guy, the *monster* of the story. But she wasn't. She didn't deserve that.

"Agree to disagree," she snapped.

"That's not going to work for me."

"I don't need you to fix me, V."

I almost said something scathing that I'm sure we both would have regretted but was interrupted when Ripley appeared at the tableside. In her hands were plates piled mostly with relatively rare meat along with some veggies and steak fries. One was placed in front of me, the other in front of Heather, before Ripley wordlessly gathered the empty bottles and walked away as silently as she'd appeared. Heather stared after her, bewilderment plain on her face, and I didn't bother suppressing my chuckle.

"If you're a wolf, you don't order here. She knows what we want, what we need."

"What if I wanted something else?"

I cocked my head to the side. "You didn't, did you?"

She stared down at her plate for a long moment, then let out an almost petulant sigh. "No. No I didn't."

I cut into my meat, sopping up the bloody juices that ran free as best I could, and asked with relative calm, "Why do you find it so hard for people to do things for you?"

"No one does anything for free."

"Your Alpha helped break your curse without requiring much more from you than your help cleaning up the mess you'd made."

"Yeah," she said, as she speared a piece of meat without cutting it and tore at it like child might. "And I'm still waiting for the other shoe to drop on that one."

"But what if there is no other shoe? You can't accept that someone might want to help just because it's the right thing to do?"

She scoffed. "Fuck no. I'm not stupid, V."

"It's not a matter of stupidity. It's believing that people might think you're worth it."

"So, Ripley knows me so damned well she can tell me what I want to eat. That goes real far in life."

I shook my head. "Now you're just being petulant."

"I'm good at it."

"It's a defense mechanism."

"No shit, Doc, am I paying for this assessment?"

I snorted into my beer but didn't push any further. She had her hackles up and almost seemed to want to argue. And I couldn't blame her with everything that she'd been through. I'd thought maybe bringing her here might help a little, that the whole thing with Ripley might make her feel more comfortable. But now I thought I'd made the wrong decision. Still, it was done, and I had to make sure I didn't risk losing her again.

"I'm not trying to *fix* you, Heather, I'm trying to show you that sometimes things are good enough to be true. We *are* mates, even if you still don't want to believe it. I want to understand, and help."

She shook her head. "There's nothing to understand or help. You deserve someone better, V. I'm a terrible excuse for a human, a terrible excuse for a werewolf, and definitely not worthy of being a mate to someone like you." She pointed her fork at me, heavy-lidded eyes focused straight at me. "You told me I showed up at the perfect time, that I saved your life. And yet here I am making things harder for you and your pack. That's all I'm good for, V, making things worse."

It was as if telling her story had destroyed whatever self-confidence she had been working on building up. I worried that whatever I said would only be met with more disparaging self-deprecation.

She was so strong and she didn't realize it. Listening to her story, reading between the lines and knowing that she survived and persevered through everything, made me want her more. It made me want her for that strength. Maybe she could help me be stronger so I could stand up to my parents better.

How was I supposed to make her understand that I didn't care about what other people in the past had made her feel? I wanted her to feel like we could have a future together. Whether with my pack, or hers, or another one altogether, I wanted to give her a life she could be proud of. But why should she believe me when she didn't think she was good enough for it in the first place?

"I don't think that's true." I held up a hand to stop her from lashing out at my words. "Sure, you being here is going to cause trouble with my pack. But that's not your fault. If anything, it's mine and my Alpha's, to be honest. We don't see eye to eye, and he made a decision that wasn't his to make for me about who was to be my mate. Now I have my true mate, so that's going to cause trouble. But I'm ready for that kind of trouble. I'm more than happy to face that trouble if it means that I get to have my true, fated mate in my life."

"But I'm not worth it."

"Who says? Your mother? We both know that she really has no idea what the hell she's talking about. Your sister? She's as bad as your mom. Who else is there, Heather? Your old Alpha couldn't care less about you at all, so you know he's not worth listening to." I spread my arms wide. "Who else, Heather? Who else sees you as nothing but trouble, as not being worth it? Does Wren feel that way about you? From what you told me, I don't think so. And I sure don't see you as trouble. Because I think you're worth everything."

"You barely know me."

"I know! Wild, isn't it?" I shook my head. "Maybe I'm

wrong. But I don't think so. And between you and me, I'd rather find out with you than take my chances and be forcibly mated to George Sinclair, of all people."

"They would do that? Force you to mate with a man?"

"I was told the night you showed up. Before I went to the hospital, my dad told me that he was going to announce my mating to Sinclair during the moon run tomorrow night."

"That's barbaric!"

"That's life in the packs, you know that."

She looked almost sheepish. "I know, but...like, I never met a wolf that was...I mean..."

"Nonbinary or not straight?"

"Well, either, I guess. That I knew of. Until I went to Terabend and met Wren. I mean, I always knew I liked— well, I mean I like both, and all and everything in between, personally. But I was also a messed-up wolf that would never be required to mate. At least that's what it felt like for the years I spent with the Cardinals."

"I have to admit that I didn't think my father would ever do something like this either. He knows I like women. He knows I don't exactly fit a typical definition of gender, that I'm an enby. That he would go so far as to demand that I mate with anyone, never mind a brute like Sinclair, was something I never expected." I glanced away. "I thought he had more respect for me than that. Guess I was wrong."

"But won't the pack take this out on you? That suddenly you're mated without considering what your father wants?"

"Sure, probably, but there's nothing they can do about it. We're mated. It's over and done with. They can't stop what's already happened."

"And there's no way to break it?"

"Break a mate bond? Not without killing one or both wolves—that I know of, anyway."

Heather finished off her steak and tucked in to munching on the fries, looking far more comfortable with this current conversation than she did when she was talking about herself. I reached out and took her hand, holding it tight as I waited until she met my eyes.

"Heather, I'm in this. Not just because you showed up at the perfect time, not just because fate decided that we were meant for each other. I want you for you, for your strength, for the young woman I think you are when you're not being overly hard on yourself. You deserve to have something good in your life, and I'm damned well going to try to be it."

Of course, the moment the words were out of my mouth was the moment the door opened and the last person I wanted to see walked into the dim light.

CHAPTER ELEVEN

Heather

My hand was warm in V's palm. Their words smashed through the walls I'd built around myself until they were so thick there was no way I could break them down. I was worth it. I was wanted. I couldn't remember the last time I truly felt that I was wanted by someone who didn't seem to have an ulterior motive.

But I guess it could be said that V had such a motive. After all, mating with me meant they didn't have to be mated to a man for the rest of their life. But the way they made it sound, the way they talked about it, that was only a bonus. The fact that I was mated to them was the most important part of it, and they seemed willing to put themselves between their pack and me should the time come.

Their eyes flickered over my shoulder and they pulled back sharply, their hand leaving mine quickly as I heard the door creak open. New scents filtered through the bar—rough, woodsy, masculine scents that sent my wolf hiding behind that stupid door she kept shutting in my face. The moment that cracked portal slammed shut the scents weren't nearly as strong, nor were the sounds of the newcomers as they came into the bar. I could still feel them moving up behind me, and if V's face was any hint, they were focused on our table.

"Don't say anything," V said so softly I had to strain to hear them. I tried to subtly show them I was listening but couldn't tell if it worked.

"Valerie!"

I flinched away from the anger that flashed in V's eyes. I did not ever want them to ever turn that look on me.

"Sinclair." V's voice had lowered dangerously but could still be heard in every corner of the bar. "You know I don't use that name."

"I don't really care." The man's voice was loud and obnoxious enough that I gritted my teeth to keep my mouth shut. The less attention I brought to myself, the better. For now. "I want to know what the hell you were doing running around with some rogue bitch instead of running with your pack last night."

My jaw hurt from clenching my teeth.

"She's not rogue." I was surprised at how calm V managed to sound with that asshole yelling at them. "She's more than welcome in our territory, and I was being a good host. You wouldn't know anything about that."

The brute was not to be outspoken. "Your father has no idea about a rogue being welcomed onto our lands! The bitch needs to pay for trespassing on our territory!"

Suddenly my chair was pulled out from under me, and I fell backward onto the ground. Rough hands reached down and grabbed me, pulling until my feet were under me but dangling in the air. I counted at least four different wolves holding me tight to allow a surly-looking, blond-haired giant of a man—Sinclair, I presumed—to level a glare in my direction.

"Let her go." I felt the wolves' hands quiver under V's

order, as if they wanted to comply but were too afraid. Was that the kind of power a man like Sinclair had over the other wolves? Fear? What a bully.

"We'll let her go when we're done with her," he snarled.

"You know there is no violence allowed in here."

"That's only for pack members, and you damned well know it. She has no say, no recourse, and no pack to protect her."

Suddenly something slammed into Sinclair's face and threw him to the side. V was there, one hand clenched into a tight fist. They stared down the other wolves.

"I said let her go."

"V." Ripley's voice was like a whiplash across the entire bar.

"I said let her go." V's words were repeated in the exact same tone. Whether or not she was worried about Ripley's warning tone I couldn't tell.

One by one the other wolves released me until I was standing on my own. I felt like I was ready to throw up, but I managed to hold myself together as V knelt down and grabbed a fistful of Sinclair's hair.

"Threaten my mate again and you won't live to regret it."

Their voice was a low snarl that made the hair on the back of my neck stand up. Holy fuck, it was kind of hot. Their hand on my arm burned for a second with the heat of anger and whatever other emotions were stirring up between us as I looked over them with new eyes. They had really stood up for me. They were willing to make themselves a pariah in their own pack for me.

They were willing to do that for me.

I grabbed their arm and pulled them to me, leaning up and forward to plant a kiss full on their lips. They were softer than I remembered from the night before and I pressed harder against them, willing them to devour me as I surrendered myself. The connection between us flared up so full that I could feel it through the barrier that separated me from my wolf. It was a moment of sensuality and comfort, a duality that made my brain spin, but I didn't care. I wanted more of it. I wanted all of it.

A moment passed with no one saying a word. I could feel Sinclair's beady eyes on us as we finally parted, foreheads touching for a second before we fully separated. V's hand stayed warm on my arm, and I allowed them to pull me away from the wolves that had been holding me and out toward the door of the bar. V stopped before we reached the doorway, turning back to all the other wolves in the bar, not only the ones who'd attacked me.

"Heather McKenna is my mate," V said, with a voice that rivaled Ripley's in her own place of business. "That is a fact. Anyone who has an issue with that can get in line and submit a formal challenge to me. But I promise that if anyone touches my mate without her express permission, I will destroy you." They glanced over their shoulder and looked at me with such primal fury that it almost made me lose my composure and launch myself at them, to hell with the audience.

"V…" I said softly, reaching out to touch their face. I couldn't help myself. I needed to touch them. I needed to stay near them. "Let's get out of here."

They smiled, opened the door, and gestured me gallantly through it. I floated out of the bar on light feet, feeling like a fucking princess with her very own awesomely badass lover-slash-bodyguard, and for the first time in a very, very long time I felt like nothing could hurt me.

This was proof that they had been honest with me from the beginning, and I needed to make good on my half of everything. If they were willing to put themselves on the line to protect me from the rest of their pack, I needed to do better at letting them in. Maybe this mate thing wasn't as terrible as I thought it might be.

Outside, the sun was setting in the early spring sky. A few speckled stars were visible if you looked from the right angles. As if on cue, my wolf roiled inside me as we walked away from that closed door, making herself known in the way she always did when we came up to the full moon. She wanted control, and if I didn't let her take over, she was going to find a way to do it herself.

"The moon is rising," I told V, who had moved their hand down to mine and was clutching me like a lifeline. I turned to look at them and realized that they were breathing rather heavily and had a bit of a wild look on their face. "Are you okay?"

They took a deep breath of fresh air. "I've never had the strength to speak against the entire pack like that before. I've done small bits of rebellion, if you want to call it that, but nothing like that. It was...intoxicating."

I leaned forward and kissed them again, softer this time and a little bit quicker. "I think that's coming from me a little bit right now."

"Oh?" They looked at me with a confused look, then blinked a few times. "Oh! Really?"

I ran a hand down their arm. "Take me somewhere safe and we might have some time to ourselves before my wolf makes herself known."

They raised an eyebrow. "All I had to do was face down the most dominant wolves in my pack to get you to want me, huh?"

"I already wanted you, V," I said, "and maybe I still want to take things slow-ish. I honestly think this is my wolf talking, but damn it, you better take me somewhere so I can rip your fucking clothes off right now."

"Yes ma'am." They led me to their bike and we got on. I nestled into their back, arms wrapped around their waist, and cheek against their shoulder blades.

What was going on with me? First it was all worry and fear and now it was like I couldn't wait long enough to get them on their fucking back. Or for them to get me on mine. I didn't mind either way. The feeling of wanting them was starting down in my core, making things warmer and warmer until it was the only thing on my mind.

So much for taking things slow-ish.

CHAPTER TWELVE

V

Heather's idea of going slow seemed to have flown out the window by the time we arrived at my apartment. I could barely pry her off me long enough to get the door open before we tumbled into my home.

I had an idea of what was going on, but I didn't want to stop things to start analyzing what was happening. She was here, she was into it, and she wanted it. And damn it, I did too. She pulled my jacket off and tossed it to the side, then went to work on my shirt. I let her do it, reveling in the touch of my mate's hands on my body. I raised my arms and let her take the shirt, then brought them down around her and pulled her close.

"I need to be sure," I whispered as I kissed up her cheek toward her ear. "Tell me."

"Tell you what?"

"Tell me you want this. Tell me you want me."

I almost cringed at the neediness in my tone and hoped she wouldn't hold it against me. I was the big strong dominant wolf who was going to protect her from my pack. I didn't have the luxury of showing weakness like that. But I needed to know she wanted me.

"I want this, V," she gasped as I brought my mouth down on her neck, giving her a little nip. "I want you. I want you."

Spurred on by her admission, I lifted her in my arms and she wrapped her legs around my waist with a yip of surprise. We kissed and caressed and touched and moved into the bedroom, where I let her fall onto the bed with a soft thump. She was on her knees quickly, her hands working on my pants. I ran my hands over her shoulders and up her neck, marveling at the beauty beneath me. My pants ended up in a pile around my feet and I pulled her up so I could pull at her shirt and pants, leaving her in nothing but her underwear.

I wrapped my hand in the hair at the back of her neck and tilted her head upward, giving me ample access to her lips and her cheek, and I trailed a line of kisses down her neck toward the healing scabs that ran down her collarbone. She gasped and whined under my ministrations and ground herself against me, pulling against my hand in her hair until she gasped in pain. I let go and she moaned like she missed it.

She grabbed my hand as she all but lunged forward, her mouth latching onto my breast and sucking greedily. Her hand entwined with mine as she moved the other to my other breast, trying to give it equal attention as I writhed with the pleasure that was coursing through my body.

"Heather!" I yelped as her teeth found my nipple in a soft nibble and I groaned, hanging my head and letting my hair fall over my face.

She pulled my trapped hand up and put it at the back of her head again.

"Pull!" she cried, with her mouth still around my nipple.

I needed no second urging as I wrapped my fingers into her hair again and slowly pulled her head back. She resisted, but I was stronger. Her own grip on my nipple was tight, and the farther I pulled her head back, the farther my tit was being pulled, until we were both gasping and ready to scream. Finally she released and I cried out as she gasped again, panting as if the same cravings that were going through my body were going through hers. I tangled my fingers tighter in her hair and came down, devouring her lips in a ravenous kiss.

"Bed?" I managed to croak when I came up for air. I was already drowning in this girl.

"Bed." Her voice cracked as I released her hair and let her fall to the bed.

I climbed on after her, staring up at her from the foot as I moved ever closer. Our next kiss was like dynamite, fireworks, explosives going off in my head behind my closed eyes. It was wonderfully right, entirely complete. Whether that was the mate bond talking or the sheer attraction I was feeling—had been feeling since I'd met her the night before—I didn't really care. We were together now, and it was absolutely amazing.

Her mouth tasted like cherry and vanilla ice cream, with only the barest hint of the beer and steak we'd eaten at Ripley's. I tasted those lips and drew a line of kisses down her neck and body. I stopped only twice, to give worship to the soft breasts that needed my attention, if the sounds she was making were any indication. I moved down and continued drawing an abstract painting of kisses until I reached the apex of her legs.

I looked up, meeting her eyes, and waited. She gave me such a warm smile of acquiescence that I wasted no more time diving in. I brushed my lips against the inside of her left leg, then her right, throwing in a slight nibble that made her gasp. Then I went for the part I knew would have her squirming all over the bed.

And squirm she did. She cried out and moved wildly

until I had to wrap my arms up and under her butt to steady her and keep my face where she clearly wanted it. She was so sensitive, more than I'd expected. But that was okay. Just more fun for both of us.

She shrieked suddenly and convulsed, her legs clenching around my head as her body writhed in my grasp. We rode out her orgasm together until she let go of my head and I pulled myself up to lie beside her. I took her lips to mine once more and she moaned underneath me, her legs shifting until a well-placed thigh made me gasp.

"My turn," she said, and worked her way underneath me. I ended up straddling her and she pulled me up toward her head. It took a few seconds, but I eventually gave her what she wanted, fitting myself right on top of her face. She went to work with a fervor that I had rarely experienced with many partners. Her movements were chaotic and unpracticed, but what she lacked in experience, she more than made up for in effort. I quickly found myself gyrating on top of her.

It was wet, messy, and by the Mother of Wolves, did I love every minute of it, as the feeling of her tongue sent the thrill of my own orgasm through me.

I reluctantly dragged myself off her and cuddled in next to her, touching her body and kissing it as she took deep breaths and came back to reality herself. Her lips met mine again and we devoured each other as we gyrated together.

It was easily, simply, one of the best nights of my life. I would remember every single moment of it.

I awoke to a panicked Heather, her back arched over the bed with her eyes closed. Her fingers were clutching the edges of the sheet in a bone-breaking rictus, her face contorted into a silent scream as I dragged myself off the bed to get a clearer idea of what was going on.

"Heather!" I shouted, but she didn't seem to hear me as

she folded almost into a fetal position. "Heather! What's going on?"

She didn't respond at all. I reached over to shake her and her mouth opened and let out a scream that made me recoil.

"Heather!"

Her eyes snapped open with another shriek of panic, and she threw herself off the bed, hard enough to hit the back wall and fall to the ground. She lay unmoving for a time, and I moved around the bed to her side.

"I'm okay." Her voice came out muffled from behind her arms and hands. I reached for her anyway, wanting to help in any way that I could. She brushed my hand away. "I said I'm okay."

I backed away from the harshness of her tone. She pulled herself to her feet, still in all her naked glory, and turned to glare at me.

"I only wanted to help."

Her look changed from something fierce to something more pitiful. "I'm sorry, V. I didn't mean to hurt you."

"What happened?"

"I get night terrors, sometimes. Not every night, but since I was a child. My mother just waved them off as nightmares. After I figured out the whole werewolf thing, they made more sense." She glanced away from me. "They're always about my wolf being caged, and when they come, they get bad."

I moved forward, and when she didn't recoil, I closed the distance between us and took her into my arms, holding her close. "I'll never judge you for that. We all have our problems, but I won't hold it against you."

She snorted. "Yeah? What's your problem, besides being too damned perfect?"

I shook my head at her. "I have issues trusting people, I

suppose. And maybe I'm a little opinionated and expect things to change when the problems in the system are pointed out. And I don't always work well with others."

She laughed. "Wow, you're really scraping the bottom of the barrel for those, aren't you?"

"Hey, you asked the question, you don't get to complain about the answer."

She melted in my arms, and I sighed as the tension drained out of both of us.

"What time is it?"

I shrugged. "Sometime around midnight, I'd guess."

She pulled back suddenly. "Midnight? But tonight is the first night of the full moon, isn't it?"

"Yes."

"And I haven't shifted yet?"

"Nope, still a hundred percent human form from what I can tell."

She looked almost lost. "Really?"

"Do you feel anything?"

She shook her head. "I don't feel her at all. Like...like being with you sated her enough not to be riled up by the moon." She looked at me as if in a new light. "And the same thing happened last night. Being around you calms my wolf, makes it easier to control her. I've never felt that kind of thing before, not even with my Alpha."

"Still," I said, "maybe we should go out for a run, let our wolves out for a bit."

"Will you stay with me?"

"Of course."

"Okay. Let's go."

We got dressed in simple, loose clothing and headed quietly out of the apartment. I led her under the cover of the shadows cast by the full moon into the ravine we'd woken up in just this morning. I pulled her to me, and we stripped each other as we kissed and touched, taking time for the tenderness of our actions to warm our hearts and our bodies, before we shifted and let our wolves out to run.

CHAPTER THIRTEEN

V

There was no dreamscape for me that night. I didn't know if Heather was there by herself, or if it was even a thing if we weren't both there. I didn't have time to worry about it. I had a bad feeling once we shifted, like something was going to happen, so I didn't let my wolf go out without a chaperone tonight.

We kept it to a mild run through the thick trees of the ravine. It wasn't the nice, open forests that one might hope for when running as a wolf, but we were used to it. You spend your life running through these types of trees and you learn to move quickly through the thin gaps. Heather lagged behind a little and I slowed to make sure she stayed close. Her wolf wasn't as present as she had been the night before, and I wondered how much in control the wolf was and if the human side of her might be along for the ride for a change.

The smell of the wolf behind me was still intoxicating to me. Like the first spring rain that clears away the heaviness of winter, she was a breath of fresh air that made me want to run faster, jump higher, and face my own fears. Those fears being the rest of my pack and how they would act if I truly spoke up against my father. Would things change if I was stronger? Or if

I were an Alpha, would I be able to make the changes I could see that we so desperately needed? I knew that a pack had troubles grouping around a wolf that wasn't an Alpha, or even a wolf that considered themselves to be dominant, but maybe it wasn't beyond the realm of possibility.

Could I convince my father to work with me until a new Alpha could be found to succeed him? Could I tell him what we needed to do to bring the pack into the present, and could I convince him to do away with some of the barbaric practices we went through?

If a wolf could scoff, that's probably the sound that came out of my muzzle then. My mate made me want to think that I could do anything, apparently. There was no way my father would ever accept me for me. I was not the Alpha he wanted. I was not willing to follow him blindly or take a mate of his choosing for pack politics. It was a foolish dream to think I could do anything to help change this pack. But maybe I could help another. Heather hadn't spoken much of her own pack, save for the bit in Ripley's bar, but it seemed small and comfortable. And had a female Alpha, which was rare. And she said they didn't follow the traditional pack hierarchies for dominants and submissives. I wondered if they had need of a strong Knight to help take care of any issues that might arise.

I let my mind wander as my wolf led the way through the ravine, imagining what it might be like to have a pack that actually cared about every member, instead of only the ones the Alpha deemed important enough to care about.

Then I caught the scent of other wolves, and I stopped abruptly. Heather caught up and stopped beside me. I recognized most of them, a party of dominant wolves from the pack. They didn't usually come this deep out of the river valley, but it wasn't unheard of. And if anything, they were probably being put up by Sinclair to follow us and get some payback for what I did to him at the bar.

He wasn't going to let that go. And I couldn't blame him. He considered himself the toughest of the tough, and I'd sucker-punched him in front of his posse. He wouldn't lie down and take that.

I pulled my consciousness ahead of my wolf for a second, directing us toward a small clearing in the trees I knew was nearby. It was far enough off the beaten path that should anything happen, we wouldn't run into any late-night joggers. Private enough for a pack of wolves even if things did get messy.

Heather seemed to notice the change in my demeanor. She still followed, but I saw how her ears lay back and her hackles rose, as if she were readying herself for a fight. For a second, I almost thought I heard her voice saying my name, but dismissed the thought quickly. She had said herself that she never rode along with her wolf, which would make it impossible to communicate with Heather directly, like we could with our wolf forms.

V? What's going on?

I started when I heard her voice in my head, spinning to look at her. I stared deep into her gray eyes, noting the slightest change from the wolf's eyes to human and back again. She was there, awake, sitting behind her wolf's eyes.

Hello, darling, I replied to her.

It was an odd form of communication shifters used only when shifted. It didn't work in human form at all, only animal to animal. It allowed our human sides to communicate when we were shifted. This was the first time I'd heard it with Heather, and it filled my heart with joy that she was awake for our run, even if there might be a hint of danger.

What is this? she asked.

You're running with your wolf, darling, I told her, *and you're awake for it. That's a good sign.*

But why stop here? And I smell other wolves.

There might be some issues. They might want payback for what happened at the bar.

She took a long moment to reply, long enough I thought she might have disappeared back behind her wolf's consciousness and was unable to answer.

I'm sorry.

For what?

Being so much trouble.

I shook my head.

No trouble at all. It could be nothing, truthfully. I'm merely taking precautions.

I couldn't say if she believed me or not, but she didn't say anything after that. She was probably more comfortable letting her wolf take the lead, and her wolf was more than happy to follow behind me. Which was good, considering the half dozen or so wolves that made their appearance from the trees at the other end of the small clearing.

My mate stood just behind and to the left of me as I faced off with the widening semicircle of wolves, all of whom had their hackles up and were baring their teeth at me. I stared them down calmly, knowing the first one to attack would be the first one to get put down.

As the first one pounced toward us I shifted, not entirely to human, but instead to the in-between form that gave us heightened strength and speed and senses beyond what either our human or wolf forms could manage. The same form Sinclair took when he'd fought that kid the other night. The form that allowed me to catch the wolf by the scruff of his neck and hurl him back into the trees. He slammed hard against a thick trunk and fell to the ground, unmoving.

The other wolves howled and moved forward, getting in each other's way as they growled in a way that was supposed to be intimidating but made me feel a little sorry for them. Another wolf leapt at me, and I ducked underneath, coming up to block the fangs of a third wolf that tried to come and bite my leg. I smashed my fist into the fourth wolf that leapt toward me, and I twisted, raking my claws across the face of a fifth. The sixth shifted into his own partial form and I cracked my knuckles, hoping this one might put up an actual fight. He threw a punch that I easily dodged, and I kicked out at his shin, slamming him right in the knee, and he fell when the joint bent backward. He screamed and rolled away, and I stood in front of them all, waiting for the next attack.

But it didn't come. Instead the wolves were nursing their wounds, and I looked around, counting them. One was missing. Sound behind me made me spin and duck at the last moment, as one more wolf went flying over my head. Heather stood back there, herself in the partial form, with a triumphant look in her eyes. I stared at my mate and felt my heart soar. She was absolutely gorgeous, and damned if I didn't want to take her again right there, but there was too much going on. And outdoor sex in the ravine was never as sexy as it seemed.

Trust me.

The other wolves were pulling themselves together but appeared to have decided not to fight us again. They slunk out of the clearing with their literal tails between their legs until the only one left was the one who'd made the partial shift. He'd shifted back to human to fix his knee but still was moving with a limp. He stared at me for a long moment.

"You're turning on your pack for this rogue?"

I shook my head. "She's not a rogue, she's my mate."

He shook his head. "Sinclair is your mate. This is just some trumped-up hussy who shouldn't be in the city." His gaze turned toward Heather. "Get out of Edmonton now while you can. We won't go so easy on you next time."

I took a menacing step toward him. "Threaten my mate again and I will kill you."

He held up his hands in surrender. "I'm only telling it like it is. Sinclair isn't going to stand for this."

"Sinclair has no say in any of this, and he certainly isn't anything important to me. Tell him that if he has issues with that, he knows where to find me."

The wolf growled something that wasn't fit to repeat in polite company and disappeared into the trees. I turned to my mate, who was busy looking up and down at herself, at her arms, her legs, like she'd never seen herself before.

"Beautiful," I said wistfully, and her eyes met mine, a savage smile creasing her lips.

"Speak for yourself." Her voice was hoarse, but still sent shivers down my spine.

"Have you never seen it?"

She looked down at her back, wagging her tail in a playful manner. "Once, and I didn't have the time to admire it. When my Alpha was kidnapped, I managed to do this, but never since."

"You think it's because of me that you're managing this?"

She shrugged. "You're the only change I've had in my life since then. I think it's a good reason."

I moved and took her into my arms, trying to comfort her and comfort myself at the same time. I'd never felt so close to someone. Damn, this mate bond was a damned thing.

"You're going to be in trouble for this, aren't you?" She asked softly.

"We'll see what happens." I held her close, taking in a long sniff of that intoxicating scent of her. "But maybe tomorrow we should go see the Alpha."

"Do you think we have to?"

"I think it's a good idea. Get things sorted out so maybe this doesn't happen again. I don't want to hurt more of my pack if I don't have to."

"I'm sorry. I didn't mean for all of this to happen. I wanted to get some closure."

"Hey, hey, this isn't your fault, okay? None of this is your fault."

"It's because we're mates, isn't it? This wouldn't be happening if it wasn't for these." She pointed at the scars on both of our shoulders.

"Don't worry about that, okay?" I told her. "It doesn't matter. Not that way. We are mates. That's what's important. If there's anyone who takes issue with that, it's on them, not us." I planted a soft kiss on the downy fur that tickled her shoulders and upper arms. "I promise, I won't let anyone hurt you. Never."

"But what about you? I don't want you getting hurt because of me either."

"I won't, darling." I pulled her tighter to me. "I won't."

I wanted to promise her that would be true, but I couldn't. There was too much risk. My father was not going to be happy about my mate coming to town, nor about the fight tonight. Outside of planned fights like the one with Sinclair the other night, fighting within the pack was generally forbidden. But there was no way I was going to allow anyone to stand between me and my new mate. Even if I had to go through my entire pack to keep her safe. It was worth it.

It had to be worth it. Because if it wasn't, then I had no idea what the hell I was doing.

CHAPTER FOURTEEN

Heather

I woke up with V again, but this time at least it was in a proper bed. Better than waking up on the leaves and undergrowth of the ravine like yesterday. I racked my brain to remember everything that happened the night before, but it felt like it was cloudy, like it was barely out of reach of my mind. First, we had come back here and had a wonderful evening, the first time I'd ever managed to do anything like that without having my wolf trying to make itself known during the act. Like being with V was a calming influence on my wolf.

Then I had one of my dreams. Well, dream was a broad term, I supposed. Night terrors, they were called when I was a child. Such a simple descriptor for something that can be so debilitating. I didn't want V to have to deal with me when I was experiencing that. It wasn't fair to them that their mate wasn't just about perfect like they were.

I held my hands to my head, trying to piece through the scattered thoughts and memories, and to remember the night before. It was like watching a movie with every fourth or fifth frame missing. Why they were fragmented I didn't know. Maybe because I wasn't used to being awake when my wolf was in control. I was only used to the odd dreamlike memory, but what I could remember from last night was definitely much more than that.

I remembered V's voice in my head, telling me I wasn't causing trouble for them. Then there were the other wolves who attacked us. And somehow I had pulled off a partial shift and helped. My wolf had allowed me to do that much for V.

Then I was here, waking up in this bed. And with my wakefulness came this overwhelming…sense of fault. I let out the slightest sob into my hands, careful not to awaken my mate. It was my fault they were fighting their own pack, my fault they were on bad terms with Sinclair, and the Alpha, and the rest of the pack. It was all my fault that this was happening, and I couldn't fix it.

Well, maybe I could. There was still a way, I supposed. V wouldn't like it, I knew, but it was the only thing I could think of to put things back to normal, to give V a better life, with their pack not one step away from attacking them all the time. V's problems weren't fully solved or anything, but with us mated they couldn't force them to mate with Sinclair anymore. V was strong enough to make anyone who might try to force their hand rethink that decision. But I was sure that they would have a better life without me, whatever that looked like for them. Maybe they'd find a new pack, a new life. Something better than being stuck with me.

The only option was simply to disappear. Go back to Terabend, be with Wren and Natalie for a while longer, then maybe leave them to find my own place in the world. My suitcase was evidence that I'd been relying on others for far too long lately, and now I was on the verge of doing nothing but the same—relying on everyone else to protect me and make sure I was safe. It wasn't fair to them, and it wasn't fair to me. I needed to learn to manage by myself, me and my wolf, without my mate or my Alpha getting involved or helping me.

That meant I needed to go back without V.

The question was how to tell them without hurting them.

I sobbed into my hands again, and this time V shifted in their sleep, turning toward me. As if they could feel me inside of them, they awoke and wrapped those strong arms around me.

"Shh, darling," they whispered softly, "it's all right. Everything will be all right."

I didn't trust my words, but I clung to their arms, sobbing openly now that they were already awake. It wasn't fair. I had found this person who would be so good for me, and now I was going to go and ruin it. I didn't deserve to have this happiness. I didn't deserve to have someone like them in my life. I needed to find a way to let them down easy, but not right now. Right now, all I wanted to do was wrap myself in their arms and know what it felt like to be loved.

I choked on a sob as the thought flitted through my mind. Love? Really? That was a strong word to use. Was this what it felt like to be loved unconditionally? Was that the way things were supposed to be between mates? I couldn't say. I didn't know what it was supposed to feel like. It was nothing like what I felt for my family, or for Wren and Natalie, whom I deeply cared for.

Was I too broken to feel love for my mate? Was that one more way that I was messed up and V was amazing? The idea only made me sob harder.

"Easy, darling," V continued to coo in my ear, "easy, easy. You're safe. You're cared for."

I noticed they were careful not to use the word *love* either. It could easily be considered too soon, since we'd only met two nights ago. What was the etiquette for that? Why was my mind thinking about that, when it could be enjoying being folded into their strong arms, and why was I worrying about whether or not they used a word that I was scared to use myself?

And here I was, only working myself into a worse fervor and sobbing even harder. And they asked nothing of me. All V did was try to soothe me and tell me I was safe.

I didn't deserve them.

I didn't deserve them at all.

It took a while but eventually I managed to calm myself down long enough that I could take a deep—if shuddering—breath. I focused on my breathing, settling down in V's arms until the flow of tears slowly came to an end and all that was left was the dry heaving and sniffling. Oh so sexy.

We stayed like that for a while, V's arms around me until I had stopped convulsing, stopped sobbing, and was able to breath normally again. I prayed that they wouldn't ask what had set me off because there was no way I wanted to try to have that conversation with them. What was I supposed to say? That I didn't know if I could be with them *after* we already did the mate bite? Not like I had a lot of say in that in the first place since our wolves were the ones who took care of all the magical mumbo-jumbo that connected two people together in a bond that outlasted human lifetimes.

Would they come after me if I left? A part of me hoped so, another part hoped they wouldn't. It wasn't fair to them to be bound to someone like me. Someone so broken that I woke up crying and couldn't tell them why.

"It's okay, darling," they said in that soft voice that made me want to turn and kiss them so damned deeply. "It'll all be okay. We'll talk to the Alpha today and we'll make things okay. Last night won't happen again. I promise."

I shook my head against V's embrace and they loosened

their hold a little. That was the exact opposite of what I wanted. I needed the strength, the warmth of those arms around me. The deep, dark spiral I was falling into was one that I was familiar with, comfortable with. But that didn't mean the thoughts I was having were totally wrong. My thoughts made me uncomfortable. They were intrusive and emotional and irrational. But I couldn't say they were wrong. I had to be stronger, but I had to be stronger for myself, not only because the people supporting me were stronger than I could ever hope to be. Sure, borrowing others' strength was an option, but that wasn't me. I didn't want to use V, or use Wren, just for their strength. That wasn't fair to anyone.

I took another deep breath. Then another. This wasn't healthy, wasn't productive. I still needed to talk to my mother, get the closure I wanted, even if it killed me. But that was something I had to do on my own, not with V.

V, whose arms around me were a source of comfort that I wasn't sure I deserved. And there they were, being the hero for me when I so desperately needed it. It was almost enough to make me start crying again, as if I had tears left for that.

We took a cab back to the hospital to pick up my car. I took the opportunity to change into something that hadn't been worn already. I settled on a loose pair of jeans and an oversized tee that would be easy to get out of if I shifted. We took my car to V's parents' house. I didn't tell them I wanted my car in case I needed to make a quick escape for whatever reason. Like their parents wanted to kill me or something so their child wasn't stuck with an absolutely broken mate. Besides other reasons they might have.

Oh Goddess, what were they going to think of me? Did it matter that I cared so much? Why did I care so much? Maybe because I wanted a family to care and like me for a change, since that wasn't something I had from my real family. But that was something I'd worry about another day. I had to get through this and then see if my mother was awake yet. Then, whether or not she was awake, I planned on heading back to Terabend—with V or without them. Would they come if I asked them to? Was that what I really wanted? I felt like there was so much confusion and frustration spinning around in my head that I didn't know what the best decision would be.

From the way V was looking at me as I drove toward her parents' house, I had to wonder if they could feel what I was thinking. Could they know what had been going through my mind this morning? Did they know I was seriously thinking of leaving them? To my self-sabotaging mind it still seemed like the best idea. Either way, the honest truth was that I couldn't stay there any longer. What that meant for V, I couldn't say, but I needed to get this done and get out of there.

"It'll be okay," V said softly, and I glanced sideways at them. "We'll be okay, I promise."

If only I had the same kind of confidence. But after yesterday and last night, I wasn't expecting anything good to come out of meeting the Alpha.

They directed me to a house in the middle of a cul-de-sac in a small community in the river valley. Somewhere I hadn't really been before but might have driven past. It was beautiful down here, with old trees lining the roads with canopies just coming to life in the early spring. The house itself was huge, a little out of the norm with the other houses in the area. It looked like parts had been added time and again to make the home bigger and bigger until it looked like a jumble of additions and extra rooms.

V took my hand as we got out of the car, and we went up the walkway together. I won't deny that I began to shake a little as we approached the front door. I had no idea what to expect in there, never mind what might happen between V and me. I wanted this to be simple, easy, but I was sure that wasn't going to be the case.

V knocked on the door lightly, and it opened almost immediately like someone was expecting us. A small woman answered the door, and I immediately noticed the resemblance to my mate. Her mom, I guessed, or maybe another relative. It was hard to say until she gave me a wide smile and pulled me forward past V and into a tight hug.

"Welcome," she said, her voice soft but her arms warm and tight, "I'm so happy to get a chance to meet you. I really am."

Her warm welcome made me freeze in her embrace, unsure of what to do. Part of me wanted to melt into her and take the motherly love I'd been missing my entire life from this potential surrogate. The other part of me had to resist the urge to say something scathing about the way her pack had treated me—and V—so far. Finally I managed to say, "Some of your pack doesn't seem as welcoming."

Frustration flitted across her face as she pulled me into the house, leaving V to take up the rear and close the door behind us. It shut with an ominous finality that made me want to run screaming back to the car.

"I'm sorry for my pack," she said. "Even as Lupa, there is only so much I can do or say to make things better. Our Alpha has been under a lot of pressure of late and is making so many difficult decisions. I'm trying to work with him to see what is going on, but it's taking time."

I tilted my head. "Is this a good time to see him, then? Or are we just making things worse?"

She shrugged. "I have no idea. But as a wolf in our

territory, you need to at least introduce yourself, especially if you're going to be staying any longer. That would still be true if you weren't mated to my child."

"Don't worry, darling," V said, as they pressed their lips to my cheek, "it'll be okay. I'll make sure of it."

"V, please don't provoke him. You don't know what he might do."

"There's nothing he can do. I'm mated to my true mate. That isn't something that can just be broken or severed."

Something flickered in her eyes before she turned that warm smile on me again and offered me a hand. "Where are my manners? I'm Terra Raines, Lupa of the Raines pack."

I took the hand softly, a churning in my stomach that had nothing to do with my wolf making me feel almost sick. "Heather. McKenna. Of the Carne pack." I hoped Wren would be okay with me using her last name for our pack name.

Terra frowned. "I don't recognize the names, yours or your pack's."

"The pack is a few hours from here," I admitted. "We control a small territory near the mountains. My name is a little more complicated. It's a human name."

Her eyes went wide. "Your parents were human?" She looked to V as if for confirmation.

I shook my head. "My mom is human. That's why she's in the hospital right now. My father was a wolf."

"Oh, I'm so sorry, dear. That must have been rough. Still, that makes you a bit of a miracle child, doesn't it? I mean, it's hard enough for wolves to conceive with each other. With humans it's rarer that anything comes to fruition."

"It's that rare?" I had no idea about any of that, but then it wasn't like I knew a lot about werewolf culture or biology, or anything.

"Were you born here in Edmonton?"

"At the Edmonton General."

She looked to V again then back to me. "Then I think our pack owes you an apology. We should've been there for you, instead of whatever else you seem to have gone through. We take pride in taking care of our pack members"—V scoffed loudly—"and making sure we find the young ones as soon as we can. Do you know who your father was?"

"No. Mother never said his name. I think…" I hesitated, remembering the memories my wolf had shared with me when we went into Ripley's yesterday. "I think he took me to Ripley's once, but I don't remember a thing about him. Mother wasn't exactly happy with the fact that he was a werewolf, and she kicked him out while she was pregnant."

"Then we definitely owe you an apology. It should never have happened that way. Truthfully, we are not as terrible as some people may make us seem."

V snorted. "Yeah? Are you going to apologize for the idiots who attacked us on our run last night?"

Terra shook her head. "You knew there were risks when you decided to parade yourself and your mate around at Ripley's yesterday. You could have gone anywhere else and been safe, but you went to our most popular watering hole, and then you broke the rules there and hit Sinclair. There was no way he would let that go."

"I knew that," V said, "but he was asking for it. In case you hadn't noticed, he's not the most intelligent person around."

"That doesn't matter, V. There is supposed to be no fighting among pack members except through sanctioned fights. You brought this on you both." She turned to me and gave me a small smile. "I'm sorry things have been so rough. I would much rather have met you in better circumstances."

"Sometimes we only get the circumstances we get," I said. I thought about everything that had gone wrong to get me to this place at this time.

V glanced at me as if worried about something, but Terra only replied, "Too true, dear." She clapped her hands and tried to seem chipper, but I could see the cracks in her facade. "But I have taken enough of your time. The Alpha is waiting for you in his study."

She led us to what I assumed was the study and knocked softly on the door. It opened almost immediately, and V ushered me inside without a word. A tall man stood beside the door, dour in a pair of dark slacks and a dark button-down shirt that had the sleeves rolled up to his elbows. His dark hair was cut short in a way that accentuated his widow's peak, and his eyes were the same brownish color as V's. It was hard to see those same eyes I loved on V instead giving me a look of intense disgust before they focused on his child.

V led me immediately to a chair and pushed me to sit. I didn't argue with them as the Alpha closed the door tightly and sauntered over to his desk, every move he made containing a coiled-up energy that threatened to spring loose. I kept my mouth shut, sure that he would pounce on me before I could get the first word out of whatever I wanted to say.

"Dad," V said sharply and drew the man's attention away from me and toward them. "This is my mate, Heather McKenna. Heather, my father, Desmond Raines, Alpha of the Raines pack."

Desmond snorted at the word *mate*, but he barely glanced at me, his beady eyes focused solely on V. He leaned over his desk, his hands holding his weight.

"You went against my wishes yet again, I see."

His voice was low and gravelly but had a cadence to it

that reminded me of V's tone, especially when they got angry. Like last night. I squirmed in my seat as I tried to focus, and not to let my mind go to happier places, like remembering V standing up for me against the rest of their pack.

"I found my true mate, what did you expect me to do?"

"I expected you to do the right thing for your pack, as I have told you to do time and again!"

"Even if that's not what's good for me? Because the pack is all you've ever cared about, certainly not your only child."

"That's exactly why I've told you what you need to do around here! Because you are my only child, and you are an embarrassment to me!"

"An embarrassment? Me? Your pack is the embarrassment! The way you control your pack and think that you can determine who should be together!"

"You are my daughter, and you will mate with Sinclair tonight. Do it and this girl will not be harmed."

I opened my mouth to say we were already mated, but didn't get a chance as V all but ripped her shirt down to show the scar on her collarbone.

"Too late, Dad."

Desmond's fists clenched atop his desk, nails digging long furrows in the wood. For a second it looked like he was about to pick the whole thing up and chuck it at us, but somehow, he managed to calm himself enough that he didn't.

"Get out," he said, his voice deceptively calm.

For the first time since we entered the house, V actually looked a little worried. They took a step forward. "Dad, I—"

"I said, get out."

V hesitated, then took my arm and pulled me to my feet. We were almost to the door when I stopped, pulled myself free, and turned toward the older Raines.

"I'm sorry," I said quickly.

He had been staring at the spot where V had been standing earlier. Now his head snapped up and his hard gaze fell on me.

"I'm sorry that this has happened, and I'm sorry that it ruined your plans. If there was anything I could do to help fix it, I would." And I meant it. It wasn't ideal, certainly, but I wanted to be able to mend things with V's family. After all, family was supposed to be important, wasn't it?

"You," he said. "You don't get to address me, you pathetic little submissive. You have no idea the kind of trouble you and my daughter have caused. The fact that she decided to find the first strumpet she could and mate them? You must've put her up to this."

I stood my ground. "Strumpet? Did you just call me a strumpet? I did no such thing to them! We are true mates, like V told you."

"Hmph, a likely story. No, my daughter was too desperate to destroy the pack that has raised her for the past twenty-eight years to bother considering what this might do to us all."

"V is your child but not your daughter! Do you not listen to them at all? They're nonbinary and sapphic! They like women! And you were about to try to mate them to a male? What kind of bastard are you?"

"You don't get to question me, peon! You are nothing! I am an Alpha! I get to decide who mates with whom, who lies with whom, and how best to keep my pack strong and together!"

"Just because they're pack doesn't mean you get to dictate their entire lives!"

"I thought I told you both to get out!" He seethed and slammed a fist down on his desk. A massive crack echoed through the room and the top of the desk snapped in half under his blow. "Go now. Leave Edmonton. Leave my pack. Because if you don't, I swear you will not like the alternative."

V took my arm again and pulled. Hard. I wanted to stay and give him more of my mind, but they were insistent, and I took it for the warning it was. I'd done enough damage to V's relationship with their father, clearly. Not that there was much of a relationship in the first place.

As we left the study, V was quick to close the door behind us, and we headed for the front door.

Terra stood at the entrance, wringing her hands and watching the study door carefully.

"Go," was all she said.

We took her at her word and left. I slipped into the driver's seat and started the engine. I turned to look at V to find they weren't beside me. Their hand was outside on the door handle, but their attention was on the house behind them. I couldn't see their face but I could make a good guess of what they were thinking. Losing one's family in this kind of way was not something that was to be taken lightly. I knew that better than most. I had hesitated that night before I ran away from my family, had looked back more times than I could remember. When the days with the Cardinal pack got really bad, I would wonder why I left at all. Why didn't I stick with the hell I knew, that I'd grown up in, rather than come all the way out here only to go through a different kind of hell?

I turned away from the door as they got in the car, but I noticed the trail of tears on their face before they could hide it from me. I pulled away from the house and watched their head hang low as if they couldn't bear to watch the house fade away into the distance. I didn't blame them. Their family was here, their pack. Everything they knew and loved was here. Their situation was complicated, and being stuck with me would only make it worse, and that was made clearer by the fight with their father.

All of a sudden, I worried that talking back to V's father might have ruined any chance of reconciliation. I wished I'd kept my mouth shut. I was sure it only made things worse. If I destroyed any chance they ever had of having their family again, I didn't know if they would ever forgive me. I didn't have the perfect family—obviously—but that didn't mean I wanted to be the reason that their family never talked to them again.

I couldn't deny just wanting to leave this all behind. Go back to Terabend, pretend like this had never happened. But I couldn't leave yet. I needed to finish what I came here to do with my mother and sister. I needed to figure out what I was going to do about V. Meeting their parents had only solidified the idea in my head that I couldn't say that I belonged with them, despite being meant to be together as mates. I needed to work on myself before I allowed someone else to be everything to me in my life.

That's what worried me the most. Getting so involved with another person as the answer to my problems was only asking for pain, if and when they decided I wasn't worth the trouble anymore. People didn't stick around out of the goodness of their hearts. And as much as V had been absolutely amazing to me thus far, how long would it be before the other shoe dropped and suddenly I was too much for them?

Even if that shoe never dropped, would they want to come with me?

Truthfully, if nothing else, I needed to talk to V. I needed to get over this mental block in my head and stop going over every doomsday scenario I could possibly think of and pull myself out of the spiral enough to talk to them. They deserved that much at the very least.

The only thing now was how they would react. I didn't

want to hurt them. I didn't want to overthink everything either. I needed them to understand where I was coming from, whether we stayed together or not. I could not say *Well, our wolves want each other, so I guess we should be together.* I was broken. Too broken. They deserved someone who wasn't.

They deserved better than me.

CHAPTER FIFTEEN

V

Heather was quiet as she drove away from my parents' house. Understandably so, I supposed. Meeting my parents was not supposed to go quite like that, but what else could I have expected? My father didn't respect me. He'd made that clear time and time again. I wiped at my eyes as subtly as I could. I didn't want Heather to see me crying over them. My father had made his position pretty damned clear. I didn't need to shed a tear for him finally deciding to show his true colors.

I don't know why I kept thinking that he'd change his mind, maybe. He had seemed interested back when I came out to him, so many years ago. Seemed receptive to my being nonbinary. To the fact that I didn't like men in that way. But over the years, it was like he'd decided to conveniently forget everything that I had said. Like he figured that it was just a phase, and he could tell me when the phase ended and then expect me to do what he thought was best for the pack.

I tried to contain my scorn, but failed. The scoffing sound I made earned a quick glance from Heather. I shook my head, wanting to keep my thoughts to myself as she drove. It'd be way too distracting for both of us if I spilled my feelings about what had taken place. I didn't need us getting in an accident.

And it wouldn't be fair to put all of this on her. She'd had no idea what she was getting into when she mated with me. Hell, she hadn't completely agreed to do that. Our wolves took care of that part for us. Talk about an awkward wake-up call. It couldn't be easy getting thrust into this kind of pack drama all of a sudden.

And yet she had tried to stand up for me to my dad. No one but my mother had ever done something like that before. Even in the face of his insults—*I mean, come on. Strumpet?*—and his bullshit, she stood up for me and tried to make him understand why we were so against his crap. Every time Heather surprised me like this, I looked at her in a new light. I knew my wolf was already predisposed to like her since we were true mates and all, but each time I thought I knew her as a human, she surprised the hell out of me and I found something else about her that I...well, that I didn't want to live without. She was so damned strong when she wanted to be, when she saw someone else being hurt. She gave me hope that maybe I wasn't stupidly jousting at windmills when I said that werewolf culture needed to change. Someone willing to stand up to the Alpha was the kind of partner I would have looked for in the first place. And here she was, falling right into my lap.

My father wasn't going to take this lying down, though. No one dared argue with the Alpha. Why would they? For werewolves, the Alpha was akin to a god, basically. There was no questioning the leader of the pack.

Which was stupid. The best forms of leadership had checks and balances to make sure that the one in control didn't have complete power. I'm not saying that we needed to figure out a democratic way to run a wolf pack, but the Alpha, my father, needed to listen to *all* of his people, not only the inner circle of sycophants who benefited from the way things were already run.

But I was tired of politics. I was tired of the pack and pack life. Maybe it was time for me to leave. Things weren't going to change. And if I didn't change to suit them, they'd eventually run me out for something else, if it wasn't this mess. I couldn't thrive here. Hell, I could barely live here. It was time for me to move on.

I wondered if Heather's Alpha had a place for me in her pack.

"I can't do this," Heather said suddenly.

"Can't do what?"

"I can't be a part of this. I can't be the reason you don't belong with your family anymore. It kills me to be the one to come between you." She shook her head. "Whatever this is between us, I'm sorry but I don't think I can do it."

"All things considered, it's a little late for that. We're already mated."

She snorted. "And whose fault is that?"

"Are you blaming me for this again? I told you it was our wolves, not me."

She shook her head. "I know. I believe you. But I don't think that I can do this. I know that you and your family haven't been on great terms lately, but I can't be the reason that what you have might never heal. I've been party to that bullshit before and I'm not doing it again."

"Heather, this isn't your fault."

"It is. I shouldn't have talked back to your father like that. I shouldn't have come back to the city, not now anyway. If it wasn't for…" She drifted off as she turned onto a street that I recognized was near my apartment. "Look, I'm sorry. I truly am. I like being with you. I like being around you, and I think my wolf does too. But I know that I am not good enough for someone like you. I'm too broken. I'm too messed up." She sighed. "I'm a monster, V. And if ever I want to fix that, I need to work on myself, not allow others to take care of me."

"Wait, wait, wait—"

"No, V, I'm not waiting. You heard me. I'm going to finish what I came here to do and then I'm going home. I know things are so damned complicated with your family. I know what it's like to have a complicated family. I lost my family when I was a child. You still have time to maybe save some sort of relationship with them."

"A relationship that leads to me being mated with and raped by Sinclair?" I snarled.

She flinched and gripped the steering wheel even tighter. "They can't force you to mate anyone anymore. We took care of that already. But maybe, given time, they can see that you are a great person and you don't deserve what they've tried to do to you. Maybe your father and you can get on the same page about changing the pack, I don't know. I know that I don't want to be the reason another family falls apart. I'm sorry I fucked everything up so badly, but there has to be a way you can make it up to them."

"Make it up to them? Why should I make anything up to them? Why would I have to? They are the ones who won't listen to me when I tell them who I am, who I want to love. Their bullshit is so ingrained that they would sacrifice their own child to preserve things the way they are."

"I'm sorry, V. I just don't know how to do this. My wolf is attached to you, but she doesn't talk to me, doesn't communicate with me. And with you...with you that's changed. Last night, I did a partial shift and was awake for the run because I was with you. But that's cheating, isn't it? It's not me being better, it's because you're around. I want to deserve you, V. I want to be deserving of someone as amazing as you are. You stood up to your pack for me, stood against your own parents for me. And it kills me inside that you had to do both because I wasn't strong enough to do it for myself."

I glanced away from Heather to stare out the window and realized we'd come to a stop in front of my apartment.

"But you are strong enough, Heather," I told her softly. "You stood up to my father for me. When he was an asshole, when he decided that he could dictate my life, who I loved, who I would be with, you stood up to him. An Alpha wolf. Was that a fluke? Or does your strength lie in helping others, even if you can't seem to help yourself?"

"That's exactly my point! I need to help myself before I can be with someone who does it for me."

"I'm not doing anything *for you*, Heather. You are changing when you're around me, because maybe a mate is what you truly want, and need, to be a more whole person. To be less broken. Sometimes it's okay to need others."

She shook her head. "I don't rely on people because there's always a cost. My life has taught me that."

"Did Wren ever demand a cost from you for breaking your curse?"

Heather didn't say anything.

"Do you think I'm going to demand anything from you besides just being with me? I care for you, Heather. More than my wolf, more than only as a mate. I truly care for you and I care that you are who you are. Yes, you think you're broken. Yes, you think you're a monster—which you really aren't. But I want to be with you. *I* want to be with *you* exactly as you are. Not later, when you learn to listen to your wolf. Now."

She was quiet for a long couple of minutes. "I don't know how to do this, V." Her voice was small, soft, and sounded more like she was talking to herself than to me.

"So that's it? You waltz into my life, I fall for you, and then you decide that we can't be together?"

She cringed away from me. "I…I'm sorry."

"No. Fuck that, Heather. You don't get to say you're sorry this time. You don't understand what I've gone through with my family. It's time I went my separate way from them, and I want that way to be with you! Don't you understand? I'm choosing you over them."

"I never asked you to do that. I don't want you to do that. What if I can't be what you need? I came here because of my need to prove myself and maybe reconcile with my family. But all I've done is destroy yours."

"But I want you. Everything about you, I want with me. My wolf wants you. I want you, Heather. Broken and all. I want you."

She shook her head again. "I'm not worth it, V. You don't understand. You say now that you want to be with me, but what about in a month? A year? Twenty years? How are you going to feel when you realize you don't have your family anymore because you chose me?"

"Heather…"

"Please, V. I might be making a mistake. Hell, odds are good that I am, desperately, making a mistake. I'm so scared that there will come a time that you decide that I'm not worth the effort, V. That you blame me for whatever happens between you and your parents, your pack. I know there are people that you care about here. I know there are people that are important to you here. I can't just take you away from them. Even if you're not an Alpha, you're strong enough to make changes in this pack. Lead them to a better future."

"I want a future that includes you," I said.

"Don't. Just don't, V. I'm going back to the hospital one more time, then I'm leaving. I'm asking you not to follow me."

"But, Heather…"

"I'm a monster, V. You deserve to be with someone better than a monster."

"You're not a monster—"

"Get out, V. Please."

There was nothing left for me to say. I got out of the car. She hesitated for a long moment as I stood on the sidewalk, watching her, hoping she would change her mind or that I could say something that would help me get through to her. I didn't think she was a monster. She wasn't at fault for the chasm between my family and me. She was perfect for me. I wanted to tell her that.

But would she listen?

She put the car in gear and drove away.

I stood alone on the sidewalk and watched my mate drive away. My true mate. Fated mate. My promised mate from the Mother of Wolves. And she just drove away.

I brushed back the tears that threatened to fall and took a shaky breath. I could still feel her in my gut, that connection that was the power of the mate bond. My wolf was going wild inside me. They insisted that I shift and go running after the car. But I didn't. I could still feel her, but she didn't want me anymore. Maybe if I gave her some time. Maybe I could find a way to make it all better. Maybe I could find a way to make her understand how much she meant to me. How much I wanted her.

Yeah. Maybe.

CHAPTER SIXTEEN

Heather

I'm doing the right thing.
I'm doing the right thing.
"I'm doing the right thing." Maybe saying it out loud would make me, and my wolf, believe it.

No. It didn't work.

It didn't work, and I guessed it wasn't really supposed to. How do you push away the person you're fated to be with for the rest of your life? I was really starting to feel something for them too. Even if it had all been sudden and mostly because of our wolves.

No, that wasn't quite right. I felt something for them the first time I saw them, before my wolf had a chance to bite. The first time their scent washed over me in the hospital room. It was everything I could have wanted in life. Almost everything. It was so close to perfect.

But I didn't deserve perfect.

I didn't deserve everything that they could give me. My family had made sure of that. I had made sure of that. I wasn't enough to have what I wanted.

I was an idiot and had ruined probably the best thing I'd ever had.

"Damn it, Heather, shut the fuck up."

Even my own voice held nothing but contempt. I hated the way my brain went down these depressive spirals. The way it drew me into this self-hatred. Mad at myself. Angry at the world. Crushed beneath the nobody-loves-me, everybody-hates-me bullshit that got so damned heavy I couldn't bear it anymore.

I had a friend once who told me I needed help from a therapist. Of course, there had been no way to convince my mother to allow me to do such a thing. And when I'd run away, I'd had nothing, no resources, no one to talk to. But my friend had been right. Maybe things would've been different if I'd had help of some sort, trying to right whatever was wrong with me. I'd focused so much on my curse after I'd learned I was a werewolf that I'd started to think that if my wolf were magically freed, then all my problems would be solved. But it wasn't that easy. It didn't work that way. Breaking the curse didn't heal years of trauma responses or abuse. The very makings of the monster I was.

V said they still wanted me. Would they still if they knew exactly how messed up I was?

I shook my head. Of course, they would. They were willing to fight their pack for me. For their mate.

I wanted to say I was unlovable, because that's what my mind was telling me. But if someone as strong and together as V could want to be with me, maybe I was wrong. I wish I could say that the heavens opened up in that moment with the light of a thousand suns, and that a choir of angels started blowing their fucking horns, telling me that I'd just had an epiphany that would make everything better.

But that didn't happen.

No. But the idea of V being honest with me before, telling me that she truly wanted me despite how broken I was, despite my insecurities, despite what my brain tried to tell me, made me want to do it all better. It made me want to turn around and go back and pick them up. To apologize to them for being such an idiot and trying to leave without them. To feel like maybe I could change the way I thought enough that I could be enough for them.

Of course, the way they played my body last night was a definite bonus.

I bit my bottom lip to stop myself from moaning at the memory as I parked the car in the stupid paid parking lot at the hospital. Last night had been amazing, except for the fight with the wolves. But before that, and even after. When V had held me in their arms...

"Damn it, Heather. What the hell did you do?" I groaned and laid my forehead against the steering wheel.

I still meant what I'd said. I didn't want to be the reason that they were estranged from their family. I knew what that was like more than they realized. I'd failed to be a part of my own family, and then my first pack was...well, I'd call it a disaster. Sure, I was wolf enough to be part of the pack, but not wolf enough to be important enough to help. That was two families I'd failed to keep. I didn't want V to know what that felt like.

But wasn't that just it? They already knew to some extent. The way their father acted—the writing was on the wall. V needed somewhere new to be, to go. They needed a new pack, one that was more in line with their ideas of what a pack should be. I shook my head again. Wren's pack sounded about perfect for them. And I'd be there too. At least, if they still wanted me.

And I had gone and screwed it all up, because I couldn't believe someone would really want me.

Okay. New plan. Finish up here, hope my mom was awake so I could finally talk to her, then go back to V and apologize. They had earned that apology more than once for what they had done last night, keeping me grounded after my nightmares and everything. Yeah, an apology was the least that they deserved.

Mind made up, it was easier to get out of the car and head into the hospital.

By now I knew exactly where to go—and I hoped they hadn't moved her. Somehow, I doubted it. She was comfy in her single-bed ICU room, and Summer would make sure she stayed that way. I slowed down at the thought of seeing my sister again. She wouldn't welcome me with open arms this time.

That was okay. I didn't need open arms. Not now. Not from her.

I entered the room without being stopped and once more reveled in the near silence. At first, I thought it was empty, but then the sullen beep of the machines gave away the fact that there was indeed someone in the bed on the far side of the room. Then the scent of my sister caught my nostrils and I paused.

She was in a chair on the far side of the bed. Her arms and head rested on the bed beside our mother. She looked like she'd been crying, but as she raised her head to look at me, there was nothing but scorn on her face.

"What the hell are you doing here? Come to finish the job?"

"Finish the job? What are you talking about?"

She sneered. "I was surprised you didn't wolf out and kill her the other night!"

"I'd never hurt her like that. Or you, for that matter."

"Bullshit. You're a monster, it's not like you care about anyone but yourself."

"Summer…"

"Don't start, Heather. You don't care a thing about us."

"Excuse me?"

Her eyes narrowed as if her glare could pierce right through me and leave me lying bloody on the floor.

"You didn't care anything about us when you left, you didn't care enough to fix yourself before you came back. All you care about are the monsters that you've been dying to be a part of your entire life."

I blinked at her for a long moment. What the hell was she trying to say? Did she really think I wouldn't have given anything to have a proper family with her and our mother? I wanted them to like me so damned badly. But I couldn't be half a person. It didn't work that way. It was killing me to try to be the person that they wanted me to be.

"Do you hear yourself? Are you seriously blaming me for leaving when she told me to leave and not come back?"

"She did not!"

I laughed scornfully. "Damn right she did! The moment I confronted her about being…" I faltered as I realized how loud we were being. "About my condition. She told me to either shut up and deal with it, or get out. I chose to get out because I wasn't about to hang around with a bitch who would do that to their child."

"Do what? Give you a chance at a normal life? Make you a normal person? She was only trying to help you."

"Bullshit! She was trying to control me and everything else in her life. Why do you think our fathers never stuck around, huh?"

She shook her head. "You know we'd never allow a monster like your dad around the family."

"We are not monsters!" I clenched my hands hard enough for the nails to pierce my palms. Nails, not claws. I didn't let the surprise cross my face when I realized that if we'd had this conversation the other day, I would've wolfed out by now. Maybe it was V's influence, maybe my wolf was giving me a break for the day. Either way, I was thankful.

Whatever Summer was about to say next was interrupted as a nurse let herself into the room. She froze for a long moment at the sight of us, then shook her head and started taking my mother's vitals. How she managed to deal with the tension in the air, I didn't know. She didn't take long to do her job, but she did pause in the doorway one last time and look back at us. I could almost see the words on her lips before she sighed and walked away.

Dealing with family drama was clearly above her pay grade. Not that I could blame her.

"Why did you come back here?" Summer asked after a long moment of silence between us.

"I wanted to say good-bye." I had to look away from her, and the bed, as I spoke. "I came here for closure, but I'm pretty damned sure I'm not going to get it, even if she does wake up at some point. I wanted to know why she did what she did, why I had to be half a person for so long because she decided it had to be so." I shook my head. "I don't know, Summer. Maybe I just wanted to have something nice to be able to say about my family."

"Get out," she said, slamming a hand into the bed beside our mother's frail body. "Get out right now. Before I call someone to haul you out."

"You think someone would do that, when I'm not the one acting like a petulant child protecting a failure of a mother?"

"She was not a failure!" she screamed.

I held up my hands as I heard footsteps running toward

the room. "Think what you want, Summer, but I know the truth. I know you don't do shit like that to a child, especially when they aren't old enough to have a say. Just because a child isn't a mirror copy of their parents doesn't make them less deserving of love."

I backed off and turned around just in time to see the nurse and a burly-looking security guard come through the doorway. I stared them down as the nurse looked back and forth between us.

"Don't worry, I'm leaving."

The nurse stayed quiet and the guard watched me go as if I were something dangerous. If only he knew the truth. Either way, neither followed me as I left, so I guess they didn't see me as much of a threat.

I didn't make it far from the room with my pride intact. Slowly, my head, which had been held high, lowered ever so slightly, and I started to feel the tears welling up. I kept my eyes down, following one of those random colored lines they put on the floor, in hopes that it would lead me back to the elevators.

"Are you okay?"

I raised my head at the vaguely familiar voice as a hand softly rested on my shoulder. The nurse from the first night I was here stood beside me, nothing but concern on her face. I wiped at my face ineffectually and turned to her.

"Yeah." That was a lie. "Yeah, I'm fine. Just…over-whelmed."

"It can be like that around here," she replied. "I remember you from the other night. I'm Trish."

"Heather."

"You want to take a walk?"

I glanced at her, ready to say no, when I caught a whiff of her scent. It smelled vaguely like V, and definitely not human.

I wasn't sure how I didn't notice before. Was this the pack maybe offering a helping hand? Was it V, working through Trish, or was the nurse just that nice that she thought I needed a walk to settle down?

Either way, I was grateful for the suggestion. "A walk would be nice, thank you."

She led the way to the elevator, and we made our way out of the hospital. She seemed to know where she was going, as we passed the parking lot and headed around the side of the building. We came up to a short walkway and a number of tables for people to enjoy time outside. Must've been a nice escape from being stuck in the hospital all the time. Despite the slight chill in the air, there were people barely clothed in their hospital gowns, sitting at the tables.

"It's not much," Trish said softly enough that no one would overhear us, "but it works for my wolf when I can't get down to the valley."

I glanced at her. She was being awfully nice, compared with how her Alpha treated me. "You come out here to shift?"

She shrugged. "Once or twice. Dire emergencies only, really. There's a reason I work the night shift."

"What do you do during the full moon?"

"I book the time off or find coverage. Or call out sick."

"And no one has noticed a pattern?"

"Not yet," she said with a shrug. "But then that shouldn't be surprising."

I chuckled as we walked past a small copse of trees. "People really only believe what they want to believe, don't they?"

She laughed with me, and we shared the moment peaceably. Out in the fresh air, things seemed a little less terrible, and my mind decided that it would start working through the rationale for what I was doing. Why was I trying to get any sort of closure from my mother? She'd made it clear what she thought of me when I was a baby, never mind as an adult, when I confronted her about being a wolf. It was ridiculous that I hoped anything might change. If Summer was any indication, my mother was probably worse than she had been before. I had never had a real family with them. I never would. Hell, I wasn't sure what a healthy family looked like. But I knew it looked more like what I had found with Wren and Natalie than it did with my mom and sister. And maybe it felt more like what I had briefly had with V.

"It's not easy to have a loved one in a place like this, huh?" Trish asked.

"Probably not," I agreed, "but whatever might be wrong with her, she's in the best place to get better. That's what hospitals are supposed to be for, right?"

"We certainly try."

"I don't even know what happened to her."

"Your mother?"

"I got the call from my sister the other night and came straight here. Like a dutiful daughter should."

"Sounds like you regret it."

"In some ways. I really think I never should have come back here. I left a long time ago for a good reason."

"Trouble with family?"

"Is there any other reason to run as far as you can when you're barely nineteen?"

"Can I ask what she did?"

I scowled and took a deep breath through my teeth. "What didn't she do? She lied to me and manipulated me. She cursed me."

"Cursed you?"

I glanced around, making sure there were no eavesdroppers. We were pretty secluded on the other side of the trees. I idly wondered if they were the same trees where V had taken me the other night to get me to shift.

"Cursed me. Literally. Locked my wolf in a cage inside me so I couldn't shift, but I could still feel her. I knew I was different than everyone else, but I never had the words or knowledge that came with it. And every time I asked about it, my mother told me that I was normal, that there was nothing different about me, and I should try being like everyone else. Everyone human."

Trish stared at me for a long minute. "Are you serious? She locked away your wolf?"

"Paid a witch to do it, from what she told me. Then proceeded to say it was the best money she ever spent. If I hadn't found out in an...incident, I still wouldn't know I was a wolf at all."

"That's horrible! So how can you shift now?"

"My Alpha. I joined her pack last year and she worked to find a way to free me." I looked away. "I'll never be able to repay her for it, but I'll be damned if I don't try."

"That sounds like a good Alpha," she said, a hint of approval in her tone.

I opened my mouth before I could think better of it. "Hell of a lot more understanding than yours seems to be."

Trish's eyebrows rose up like she couldn't believe I was being mildly insulting to her Alpha. After the shock, she settled, though, and gave a little shrug.

"He's been the Alpha for a long time. He's a little set in his ways."

I snorted. "That's one way of saying it."

She opened her mouth to speak but was cut off when a phone beeped loudly. I reached for mine, but Trish was fast, pulling hers out and glancing at the screen before mine was out of its pocket.

"Shit." She looked up at me. "Look, I think you're really nice and you don't deserve what's going on, really you don't."

"What?"

"For what it's worth, I'm really, really, sorry about this."

"About what?"

"About this," a new voice announced behind me. I spun, ready to run, to shift if I had to, but Sinclair was too big and strong. Right behind me, he was quick to grab my wrists. I struggled against him, but couldn't make any headway as several more of the wolves I recognized from his posse at the bar yesterday closed in around us.

"What the fuck?" I pulled one arm free, only to find myself being held by one of the other wolves. I glanced over my shoulder, but Trish was already out of reach and backing farther away, her hands over her mouth. "Get the fuck off me."

"Not a chance. You don't get to waltz into our territory and take whatever you want."

"What are you talking about?"

Sinclair grinned. "We're going to see just how strong a mate bond is."

I felt the sudden rush of fear flood through me, and I tried to pull myself from their clutches, but there were too many of them. I opened my mouth to scream, but one of the wolves at my back was quick to cover my mouth. I bit down hard the second I could get purchase on the hand, and he howled and backed away.

"Damn it! You couldn't do this the easy way, could you?"

"Fuck you!" I screeched. "V! V!"

"Shut her up!"

"V!" I cried out before something hard smashed into the back of my skull and everything went dark.

CHAPTER SEVENTEEN

V

I finished off another bottle of beer and opened a fourth, taking a swig before it joined the others on the table beside my armchair. The problem with trying to drown your sorrows as a werewolf was that alcohol wasn't all that effective for getting a really good buzz on. Not unless I drank it by the keg.

Which I only did once and realized three kegs in that it was very much a mistake.

But I thought that maybe enough alcohol might help to numb my heart if nothing else. I could still see the look on her face when she told me she was done. That she didn't want me. She'd rather I stay with a toxic family like mine than risk coming between me and them.

She didn't understand that there was no way she'd ever come between me and them. I would always stand against them *with* her. She was my mate. My true mate. Fated mate. Whatever the hell werewolf lore wanted to call it, she was mine and I was hers, and we belonged together. I couldn't figure out why she didn't feel the same way.

But I wasn't going to crowd her. Maybe—hopefully— she'd come to her senses before she left town. I wasn't fully certain where her pack was. Somewhere called Terabend, she'd told me. A few hours west of here out toward the mountains.

Just the thought of the wild forests one might find out there made me interested enough that I got up, forsaking my beer and heading for my laptop. It didn't take long to locate the town. Nestled in the middle of nowhere, between the mountains and a giant lake in western Alberta. Sounded peaceful, to be honest. Better than trying to hide out in a dense river valley.

I was trying to imagine it. Old, wild forests where we wouldn't risk stumbling across a group of mommy-and-me joggers. Wide open spaces where we could run under the light of the full moon. It sounded like heaven to me.

I could follow Heather. Her pack seemed different. It made me wonder why I hadn't thought of leaving my own pack before. There was a simple answer to that: I didn't know if what I would leave them for was any better than what I already lived with. The devil you know, and all that.

One second I was lazing in my armchair, wondering what a new pack might be like. Then suddenly I was on the floor, pain radiating from the back of my head. I raised my hands, trying to feel for a wound, but there was nothing there. But inside me, my wolf was howling in pain and fear and desperation in a way they'd never done before.

"Heather," I murmured. I held a hand to my chest and tried to find that still tenuous thread that connected me to my mate. Something had happened to her. Something bad enough that it shunted what she was going through down the connection into me. I clung to that connection, barely strong enough between us to feel it. I needed to know what was going on.

I had my phone in my hand before I could really think about it as I tried to remember Heather's words from the bar yesterday.

"Wren," I said softly, "her Alpha's name was Wren. She owned...what was it again? A bar? No, a diner."

When I found the number, I punched it in, wondering if I was doing the right thing.

"Thank you for calling the Tooth and Claw Diner," a cheerful voice said from the other end.

"Oh...uh...hi," I stammered slightly before I puffed myself up and shook my head to clear my thoughts. "Hi, I'm looking for Wren."

"Just a moment." The sounds of plates and silverware clattering was muffled further for a second before a new voice came on the phone, this one strong and at ease.

"Wren here. How can we help you?"

"Is this line secure?" I asked softly, hoping she would understand what I was asking.

"Hold on." A beep sounded and the line went dead. I had to hope I was only put on hold and not hung up on.

Why was I doing this? What did I hope to gain? I had no idea. I needed to know where Heather was and what had happened to her. If there was anyone who might know, it might be her Alpha. And truthfully, I wanted to know about Wren and her pack. I needed to know if I could have a place where I would be appreciated, not used.

"Speak." Wren's voice came back over the phone, brusque and full of worry this time.

"My name is V. I'm the Knight of the Raines pack in Edmonton."

"Is this about Heather?"

I hesitated. "Yes."

"Is she in trouble?"

"That's the problem. I don't know."

"Speak plainly, please. You reached out to me, clearly you want something."

"Heather and I…we mated. She is my true mate."

There was a long moment of silence on the other side of the line.

"I'm listening," Wren finally said, though I couldn't pretend I didn't hear the growl in her voice. Was this Alpha like my father? Not caring about fate?

"I haven't seen her since this morning, near noon. But a moment ago I felt something through our connection and it… well, it scared me. I'm worried about her. My father is the Alpha of my pack, and he doesn't approve of my mating with Heather. I'm worried that he will do something or has done something already."

"If you're mated, why are you apart right now?"

I let out a long sigh. "Because she got scared and tried to tell me she was too broken for me to be with her. She told me she needed time. I wasn't going to deny her that. I…I care about her."

"Damn it, Heather," Wren muttered on the other end of the line. "She has a habit of self-sabotage. I think it's one of the reasons she has so much trouble with her wolf."

"She is having a lot of trouble with the connection between us. Her wolf is all in, but she doesn't think it's going to work."

"And if that changes? If she does decide that she wants you?"

I faltered at the direct question. But my answer came quickly enough.

"I want her, Wren. I need her. She has so much strength in her and gives me the courage to be more and do more than I ever could without her. I wish she could have an idea of how strong she really is. I want her to believe how much I need her."

"She's her own worst enemy sometimes," Wren said, then went silent for a long minute. "And do you want a place with her when she comes back to Terabend?"

I closed my eyes and let out a small breath. "Yes."

"And you're willing to leave behind your pack and your loyalties to them?"

"More than okay. I've recently come to realize that I can't change how our pack is run here. Maybe a different pack with a different Alpha might be a better idea." I paused for a moment then added. "And I'm not welcome here. Not as I am. I'm nonbinary, but my father refuses to accept it. I want a pack where I am respected, not ignored."

"Your father isn't accepting of who you are?"

"No. Not at all."

A soft sigh came over the line. "If you both agree, then there is a place here for you." The moment I heard those words I let out a long breath. "But for that to happen we need to know where Heather is."

"I thought she was heading back to Terabend, to you."

"No. I didn't know she was coming back yet. I haven't talked to her since she left."

"Fuck." I tapped the phone against my forehead as I tried to think. "I mean, I could be panicking for nothing, but I feel like something happened to her. Something bad."

"I'm getting that feeling too, but it's not as strong as your mate bond," Wren said. "Trust your bond. If you feel like something is wrong, then something is wrong."

"I don't know what to do."

"I'm on my way. We'll be there in a couple hours, sooner if I can swing it."

"Wait, you're coming here?"

"I'm coming to collect my wolf, and you, if you choose."

"Are you sure it's wise to leave your territory?"

That made Wren laugh. "There's plenty of folk here willing to defend the county if I need to leave for a little while."

I gave her my address, and the address of my father—just in case.

"I hope calling you was the right thing."

I could almost hear the Alpha baring her teeth toward the phone. "I'll protect my wolves with my life. Heather is mine. You did the right thing."

The line went dead.

Her words were only mildly reassuring, but having some sort of backup when it came to Heather—and standing between her and my father or Sinclair—was for the best.

I spent the next hour or so pacing my apartment, clutching to the feeling of my mate through our bond. She was still alive, that was the most important thing, but I felt impotent in attempting to find her. I could have gone to the hospital, torn the place apart until I found her, but I didn't want my father to have a reason to send his wolves after me. Abusing my position in the pack was not my idea of a good time. I hoped whatever might have happened had nothing to do with my father, but I couldn't help but suspect him. Still, I needed proof before I could go after him.

My phone pinged on the table, and I raced across the room for it. Not Heather. Instead, it was a text message from Trish. Another 9-1-1 text from the hospital. I stared at it for a moment. Was it Heather? Was she in danger of shifting again, or was it something else this time?

Either way, I didn't have time to waste. I grabbed my jacket and raced out the door to my bike, revved it up, and peeled away from the apartment.

When I reached the hospital, Trish was by the front door, pacing back and forth. She looked up when she heard the roar of the bike and watched me closely as I parked to the side and turned the bike off.

"V! I'm sorry. I'm so sorry."

I shook my head, looking around for whatever was the issue. "Sorry? For what?"

"They came, and they made me do it, and I didn't want to, but you know I can't say no to the dominants and—"

"Trish!" I snapped, already feeling the anxiety rising in my throat. "I need you to calm down a little and tell me what is going on."

"It's Heather! They took her."

"What?"

"Sinclair and his crew! They took her!"

"How?"

She shook her head. "I'm sorry! They made me do it."

It took a little more prodding, but eventually she told me everything. I resisted the urge to do something drastic, telling myself that she didn't have a choice. Not with our pack. I cursed both Sinclair and my father under my breath.

"Enough," I said to stop her blabbering. "Enough, Trish. Where did they take her?"

"I don't know. I wasn't—I wasn't supposed to contact you."

"My father knows about this?"

"He's the one who gave the order."

"Motherfucker," I snarled.

I spun and headed back for my bike. The engine roared as Trish called over it.

"What are you going to do?"

"I'm going to get her back!"

And my father was going to have some explaining to do.

CHAPTER EIGHTEEN

V

I broke several traffic laws on my way to my parents', but it didn't matter. The only thing that mattered now was finding Heather before Sinclair and his crew did something to her. Whatever he was planning, I had to stop it. I had promised no one would hurt Heather, and I wasn't going to let anything happen to her. I knew this had come down from my father. I didn't know his plan, but he had a hand in it. And I needed to get answers from him.

I didn't bother to knock this time. I almost kicked the door down but decided to see if it was unlocked first. It swung open as I was reaching for the knob, my mother standing there like she was expecting me.

"Where is he?" I demanded.

"In his study, why?" she asked.

"He took her."

"What?"

"He took my mate!"

Her brows furrowed. "No, no, he wouldn't do that."

I moved around her and headed for my father's study.

"He did. Gave the order to Sinclair, forced Trish to get her out of the hospital so he could grab her."

"Your father wouldn't do a thing like that." She trailed after me.

I wished I couldn't hear the lack of confidence in her tone, but it was there. Like she didn't fully believe what she was saying. It seemed a very real possibility that she didn't know her husband well at all.

"I'm not playing around, Mother. He took her, and now he'll answer to me."

She tried to say something, but her voice died the moment I kicked open the door to the study.

I stormed in, knowing I'd find him exactly where he always was, behind his desk, looking entirely unperturbed by my entrance.

"Where the hell is she?" I screamed at him.

"Lose your mate already?" he said calmly, steepling his fingers as he stared at me over them. "I guess it wasn't *meant to be* after all."

"Don't give me that shit. You sent Sinclair after her! You know exactly what is going on and where she is."

He shook his head. "You don't understand anything, do you?"

"I understand that you're a selfish piece of shit who wants everything your way and can't stand when the world doesn't work the way you want it to!" I took a deep breath, trying to calm myself a little, before I did something more drastic than kicking my way into the Alpha's study. "I want her back."

"She's not good enough for you."

"That isn't for you to decide. Heather is amazing. She sees me for who I am. She *respects* me for who I am. She is a better person *and* a better wolf than you or anyone else in this pack. She has more grace and strength in her little finger than you have in your entire being!"

"You are my daughter! I am your Alpha! I will choose

your mate and you will give me heirs. And if the Mother is willing, they will be Alphas who can take over the pack when I am ready to step down."

"The Mother has already given me my true mate! And I am not your pawn. This culture is ridiculous. You judge wolves for all the wrong reasons and in all the wrong ways. You enforce a stupid dominant-submissive dichotomy that keeps the more peaceful-minded of us down while celebrating those who are willing to kill each other. The bloodthirsty get more say and wield more power, and it's disgusting. It's no wonder people think of us as monsters! It's such archaic bullshit."

"This is the way things have been done for centuries. You don't understand how far back our line goes, how important it is that we keep it strong by making sure you mate with a strong dominant." He stood up from behind the desk and slammed his hands down on it, finally showing some temper. "I will not allow a wayward child such as yourself to be the end of my line!"

"Go fuck yourself!" I took a challenging step toward him. "The world we live in has changed, and the pack needs to change with it. You can't expect everyone to stay in line through fear, through bullying and coercion. Things need to change."

"There is no Alpha in any pack anywhere that would dare try to change the way we live. We have survived for centuries by ensuring our packs are the strongest they can be. There are no more wars between packs because we are each strong and tight, because of the way we do things. You refuse to understand why we do the things we do."

"A pack run through respect instead of fear can be just as strong, if not stronger."

"Any Alpha that attempted such a thing would be a

laughingstock! They'd be overrun and killed by the first wolves who wanted their territory."

I opened my mouth to continue arguing when someone cleared their throat. I spun. In the doorway stood two women, one tall with short, spiked silver hair, the other shorter with long ginger locks.

"Did we come at a bad time?" the taller one asked, her voice full of fury and snark. I did a double take, recognizing the voice I'd heard on the phone only a short time ago.

"Who the hell are you?" my father demanded of the newcomers.

"Wren Carne. Alpha of the Carne pack." I noticed the slight hint of distaste that colored her tone when she announced the name of her pack but didn't say a thing. She gestured to the woman beside her. "This is my Lupa, Natalie." Natalie gave a slight nod to my father, the only bit of deference either of them showed. "My wolf, Heather, came to Edmonton a couple of days ago to visit her sick mother. Now I hear she is missing. I would like to know what is going on."

"I don't know anything about the girl," my father said quickly, as his eyes flickered between the three of us. He wasn't prepared for reinforcements.

"Bullshit!" I growled. I walked up to Wren and held out my hand. "I'm sorry we have to officially meet this way. I'm V. Heather is my mate."

Wren gave me a warm smile and shook my hand. "It's nice to meet you in the flesh." She cocked her head. "They, right?"

I matched her smile. "That's right. Appreciate the ask."

"I respect the wolves in my pack," she said in a flat tone, as her eyes moved back to my father. "Any Alpha worth their salt should do the same."

"Why are you here, Alpha Carne?" he all but yelled into the room.

The only person who wasn't staring at him with dislike was my mother, who instead studied him like he was a new person. Like she had never seen him before.

"I told you why I'm here. Are you purposefully being obtuse?"

Natalie put a hand on Wren's shoulder.

"Perhaps he simply didn't understand, or doesn't remember," she replied, her voice bright but strong. "I mean, for a big, strong Alpha like himself, I'm certain that he has many issues that he has to deal with daily. He couldn't possibly remember if a wolf came by to see her sick mother."

Somehow Natalie's sweet voice was more of an insult than any words that came out of her mouth, and I could see my father's fingertips scratching the surface of his shiny new desk in anger.

"Yes," he said through clenched teeth. "I met with her this morning, alongside my daughter."

I sneered at him as he said *daughter* and noticed Wren's hands clench into fists with the word. Wow, she really did care about that kind of thing. Already, hers seemed like a pack that I could finally be happy in.

"Then where is she?" Wren asked.

"I don't know! I told them both to get out of my sight and they left! The last thing I heard was that she was headed back to the hospital—"

"Enough!" my mother snapped, loud enough to silence the entire room. She turned on my father. "You are lying through your teeth, and I can't believe you would do something so… so…callous!"

"Terra, please."

"No, Desmond. This has gone on long enough. You had

no right to interfere with our *child's* mate, the wolf they are meant to spend their life with. Now tell them what you are doing and where the girl is!"

"I will not be contradicted by my own—"

"Desmond! You will tell them what they want to know, or I swear I will make sure everyone in the pack knows just how weak you truly are."

I looked back and forth between my parents. If that wasn't a damned bomb, I didn't know what was.

"Alpha? Dad!"

He shook his head. "Don't you dare say a word!" he growled, but his anger seemed to have run out, leaving his words empty and kind of pathetic.

"Where is she?" Wren demanded.

My father bared his teeth at her but focused on me.

"I thought you were mates. You can't feel where she is?"

He wasn't wrong. I should be able to feel her. But that connection between us was tenuous at best, probably because of the communication issues with her wolf. But I knew better than to seem weak in front of my father. I stared him down instead, letting his comment fall away as uselessly as his earlier bravado.

"Where is she?" I asked one more time. It felt like we were tiptoeing through a minefield, where one wrong move could make everything blow up in our faces.

"The old grocery store. The one off Ninety-Seventh Street. Been closed for ages." He shook his head. "Sinclair is there with his crew. They're holding her until the witch can get there."

"What?" I asked.

"Witch?" Wren asked, at the same time.

"What are you planning to do?" my mother said into the shocked silence.

"The witch has handled wolves before," he said slowly, refusing to look me in the eye. "He is going to break the mate bond without killing Valerie. Then she can mate properly, with Sinclair."

"And what will happen to Heather?"

He shrugged. "I don't really care. If she perishes in the attempt, so be it. As long as my little girl is free to mate with my Enforcer. With the mate I have chosen for her."

I stormed up to my father, grabbed the side of his desk, all pretty and new after the argument this morning, and threw it in the other direction, leaving nothing between us but a handful of papers that fluttered to the ground.

He stared at me like he'd never seen me before.

"You son of a bitch!" I roared and smashed my fist into his face. Him crashing to the ground barely made me feel better. Maybe a little. "I will never, ever be your daughter, or do what you wish. Ever again."

"You don't understand," he mumbled. "You don't know what I've done for this pack."

I knelt down and grabbed him by the front of his shirt. "And I don't give a shit. You tried to use me, to sell me like I was nothing more than a piece of meat. You refuse to accept me as I am. I will never, ever forgive you for that."

I let him go, and spun, heading for the doorway that Wren and Natalie still blocked. "C'mon, I know where she is. We need to get her now."

Wren followed me, and Natalie trailed behind us. As we left the house, I turned to Wren, who took the lead and headed for what I assumed was her Jeep.

"Are you sure you want to do this?"

"I came here to get my wolf back and collect you as well," Wren replied. "That's exactly what I plan on doing."

"But this isn't your problem. You could go back home and forget about me, about Heather, all of it."

"What kind of Alpha would I be if I ignored my wolves when they are in trouble?"

"Not a very good one."

She shook her head. "No, not a very good one at all." She stopped at the door to the Jeep. "Listen, Terabend is a lot different than what you're used to. I don't only mean my pack, either. The entire town is different. We're a sanctuary for all sorts of supernatural peoples. More than just werewolves. And if you can't handle that, I need to know now. Before there's any kind of trouble."

I shook my head. "I can handle it, Alpha." The word stuck on my tongue a little, and it looked like Wren winced at the title. "Different is exactly what I need."

"Get in the passenger seat," my new Alpha ordered. "You can direct me from there."

I glanced at Natalie, who was already climbing into the back. "Your Lupa is okay with that?"

"Easy, V," Natalie said softly, "we don't stand too much on ceremony, to be honest. Just get in and we'll go get Heather."

I took a deep breath and did as they asked.

This is going to take a lot of getting used to.

But hey, I was game. I wanted something different, and it looked like now I was going to get it. I settled in the front seat and focused on the thread that connected me to my mate. It was still stretched tight, and I could barely feel a thing, but the panic and fear was still coming through.

I was going to find her and rescue her. If nothing else, I would make sure no one ever hurt her again. I'd promised.

CHAPTER NINETEEN

Heather

I woke up in a cage that was far too small for me, and for the first time in my life I knew I felt exactly what my wolf had been feeling for all those years. The metal bars were close enough together that I had to turn my hand and flatten it to reach through, and only up to the wrist. My first thought was surprisingly rational. I wondered exactly what was usually put in a cage this small. Then it kicked in that I was locked in the cage, and I started to panic. I kicked and screamed at the bars, but to no avail. Everything was solid on this damned thing, and no one came running when I screamed as loud as I could.

I was alone in every way that I could think of.

I struggled to turn myself around, trying to get off my back and stretch out some of the kinks in my legs from being unceremoniously shoved in here. I ended up on my hands and knees and felt like very much the definition of a dog in a cage. I screamed again, wordlessly, hoping that someone, somewhere might hear me. But it was quiet and no one seemed to be around. It kind of upset me that I wasn't worth guarding.

And then there was the moon. I couldn't see it, but I could feel the full moon rising outside. It was like a constant buzzing in my head, and an itch that was slowly moving up my body, as the moon rose higher and higher. I sat back on my haunches, my head bent against the bars at the top, and I closed my eyes, seeking some sort of connection with my wolf.

It was like she was waiting for me. I could feel her stirring and fretting inside me, driven by the moon and the panic and fear of being locked in a fucking cage. I wasn't afraid of her this time, though. I realized for the past months I'd done nothing but greet her with fear, every time we shifted. I was afraid of being a monster, like my mother told me I would be. I was scared of my wolf. And I had spent so long vilifying her and blaming her for a childhood spent as half a person when it was never my wolf's fault.

It wasn't mine either. I had to forgive my wolf and find a way to forgive myself. We were both victims of my mother's cruelty. Well, not anymore.

"We need to talk," I whispered. I couldn't smell anyone around me, but I wasn't sure this was a conversation I wanted others to overhear anyway. "I'm sorry."

My wolf stirred inside me more, perking up her ears as if to say, *I'm listening.*

"It sounds pretty lousy to make this an *it's not you it's me* speech, especially when we can't exactly break up, but it's the truth." I took a deep breath, wondering if I sounded like I was being irrational, or if talking to myself was the way to go here. "I blamed you for it all. If you didn't exist, I wouldn't have been cursed. I wouldn't have had this…half-life of mine."

At that she seemed less inclined to listen.

"Wait!" I all but shouted. It got her attention, before she closed the connection between us or decided to take over, as she had done on the previous full moons we'd been through. "I get it now. I understand what I did, and I promise, I'm not going to blame you anymore. I want to work with you. Be with you. We share a body, don't we? I want to embrace you and have you embrace me. Not literally, of course, because that would be a weird thing, but—" I shook my head. "I'm getting way too deep into this."

I could feel her almost chuffing inside me, like she was laughing at my run-on bullshit.

"Look, can we work together? I want to share with you, our feelings, our connection. I want what the other wolves have. I want to know you and be known by you. Does that even make sense?"

It was really hard to gauge her reactions to my one-sided conversation, but it seemed like I was getting somewhere when she suddenly threw open that barricade that kept us apart and I felt everything she was feeling.

I cried out from it. The hurt, the pain, the anger. Basic emotions that my wolf felt all the time, because she was blamed for things she had no control over. How I treated her—it was no better than the way my family had treated me.

"I'm sorry," I gasped through the torrent of emotions. "I'm so sorry."

I leaned over and let the wolf inside free, calling forth the change willingly. No panic. No fear. It was the smoothest shift I'd ever managed, despite the confines of the cage. My body swelled with a power that I'd only felt twice before, months earlier when my wolf was first released. If I hadn't been so afraid of my wolf, I could've felt this way sooner. But that was a lamentation for later. Right now, I needed out of this tiny cage.

We pawed and clawed at the bars with new strength, turning our head sideways to grip them in our teeth. Slowly but surely, the bars bent and broke under our savagery, and we leaped free from our confines as yelling erupted through the building.

"She's loose!" a voice shouted, and we turned toward it, sensing him by scent and hearing and sight all at once. It was as if we saw a target on his back. And we went for it.

He was slower than we were, and our pounce took him down to his knees. We struck with deadly precision, and ripped into the man's throat before he could do more than scream. More voices and footsteps entered the large open room, and we dashed forward toward another target. This one was quicker, shifting to his own wolf form and dodging out of the way of my strike. We circled each other for a few seconds, growling and snarling.

I could feel the saliva dripping from our mouth. It was such a rush, an amazing feeling to be present in my wolf and working with her instead of being afraid.

Then, as we lunged toward the wolf that was baring its teeth at us, everything stopped. We hung in midair and the wolf we were leaping toward sat back on his haunches, chuffing like he was letting out a laugh.

"No, you don't, little one."

The words came from behind us, but we couldn't turn around. The voice wasn't familiar, but something told me I'd heard it before. Like a long time ago, a memory that I shouldn't have. My wolf felt the same, the scent of the newcomer was something that tickled in ways I could barely describe.

The wolf we were facing off against shifted back and was quickly joined by Sinclair, who was glaring at someone behind us.

"It's about time you got here, Ritten," Sinclair spat.

"I can leave if you'd like," the voice—Ritten—replied. "I have no skin in this game. I do not need to be here."

"If you leave, you don't get paid."

Laughter boomed behind us. "If you think I'm scarce on funds, you'd be mistaken." A figure stepped around us and we were left staring at his back and outstretched hand. "You might be surprised how many people are willing to pay for my services."

"I don't really care," Sinclair replied, "as long as you can do what you say you can do."

The man decided then to turn around and look at us. His eyes traveled up and down our body, still suspended in midair. His mouth cracked into a wide smile, showing a tooth capped in gold that reflected the low light of wherever we were.

Something niggled in the back of my mind, like we knew this guy from somewhere. He was taller than me, but that wasn't hard, and had shaggy brown hair. He wore a long leather overcoat, like he'd walked out of a western or something, with jeans and hiking boots underneath. His shirt was plain black, blending in with the jacket. I racked my brain, trying to figure out where I knew him from.

Ritten gestured with his hand and suddenly we were moving, coming to rest on the ground in a sitting position. We still couldn't move a muscle, so we seemed to be sitting all docile and sweet. I hated not being in control of myself, but my wolf was going berserk inside of us. She didn't understand what was happening, only that someone—this Ritten person—had some sort of power over us.

"You want to break a mate bond without killing your Alpha's offspring, right? I can do that. Can't guarantee this one will survive, but you don't seem to care about that."

We struggled against whatever hold he had on us, but his hand was still held out, and the power he wielded still kept us frozen.

Sinclair moved forward and grinned. "No, this one doesn't matter. It's the other that's the Alpha's daughter. She must survive no matter what."

"Yeah, yeah." Ritten waved his other hand. "I got it." He took a step closer to us, still eyeing us up and down. "I feel like I know this one. I've seen her before."

"As far as we know, this is her first time in the city."

He laughed. "No, wolf. She was born here. She had a mother who had a lot of money."

We tried to growl and throw ourselves at him but couldn't move.

"What are you talking about?"

He shook his head and flicked his finger at me. Suddenly I could move again, but something was different. I looked down at myself and saw nothing but my naked body and the tatters of the clothes we'd shifted through.

"You son of a—"

Sinclair and his crony rushed forward, grabbing my arms before I could launch myself at Ritten.

"Tell me, girl," he said, calm, like he was threatened by naked women every day and didn't care. "Do you remember?"

"I know you."

"So, you do remember."

I shook my head. "No, but I recognize your scent! You're the one who cursed me in the first place!"

He clapped his hands, and suddenly I was on the ground again, torn from the other men's arms. "Very good! I was hoping you'd get it right." He chortled. Then he moved toward me again and lifted my chin with his hand to look him in the eyes. "I guess my question now is…who destroyed all my hard work?"

"Fuck you!" I tried to spit at him, but my jaw clamped shut

before I could get the saliva out. Inside, I could feel my wolf, but only at a distance, like she was locked back in that cage where she'd spent so many years. I wanted to free her. Needed to free her, but there was nothing I could do against this power. How did Ritten have such power over werewolves? Was he that strong a witch? What I wouldn't have given to have Rias nearby. She'd freed me before. She could take on this pathetic excuse for a person.

"Rias?" he asked.

I stared at him. Had he read my mind?

"Is that the witch who broke my enchantment? She must be pretty powerful."

"More powerful than you could imagine!" I growled. "If she were here right now, she would eat you alive!"

"This is all very interesting," Sinclair said before Ritten could respond. "But are we going to do this or not?"

Ritten stuck a finger in his mouth and held it up as if testing the wind. "Soon. The moon isn't quite at its apex. The ritual works best with the moon at its highest point."

"Can she shift?"

He laughed. "Not a chance. Tie her up and toss her somewhere. We'll need her soon."

Where they pulled the silver manacles from I had no idea. They were lined with soft fabric that prevented the silver from touching the skin. I was thankful that I wasn't in constant, burning agony. Instead, I was left beside the remnants of the cage, my legs and wrists hogtied together. I reached for my wolf again, but it was like butting my head against the sides of that cage—useless and only resulted in a headache.

Tears started falling when I felt her pain through what little connection we managed. I clung to her as best I could, putting everything I had into staying close to her.

You're not alone. I needed her to know. *We'll get out of this. You aren't alone anymore.*

Somehow, as much as the words were meant for my wolf, they evoked images of V, and I felt them like I felt my wolf. I knew I wasn't alone anymore, either. V was coming for me. They said they would always be there. And for the first time in a long time, I felt like I could actually trust that.

CHAPTER TWENTY

V

I started fidgeting the moment we started moving. I had to get to my mate. There was no discernable change in that thread between us, but I knew something was happening. Something bad was happening to her, and I needed to be there to help her. I needed to save her, if it was the last thing I did.

How much of that was me and how much was my wolf, I wasn't sure. My wolf was insistent that Heather and I belonged together forever. I fervently agreed with them. Often, feelings like this can take time to develop for our human halves, but I was already so deep in this, and I knew it was true. We would be together in the end.

But whether it was my wolf or me didn't matter much, did it? Heather was in danger, and I needed to help her. I was going to save her. I had promised her no one would hurt her, and I wasn't going to break that promise.

"Drive faster," I said to Wren.

The Alpha wolf looked like she didn't want to take orders from me, but I think she understood the situation enough to know not to try and argue as she pressed down a little harder on the accelerator.

"I won't let anything happen to her, I promise," Wren said. I believed her.

In the back seat Natalie was fidgeting almost as badly as I was, but not for the same reason. I glanced back at her to see her scratching at her arms and legs through her clothing—a loose sundress that looked similar to the one Heather had worn the night we met.

"Is she going to be okay?" I asked Wren, worried now that I had pulled the Alpha and her mate out of something important to help me with Heather.

"We were attacked last year. Natalie was almost killed and I turned her. She's still new at the transformations during the full moons."

I stared at the Alpha for a long moment. She'd turned a human? I knew Alphas had that power, but I'd never heard of anyone using it before. I glanced back at Natalie again and winced. The full moon had much more influence over her, and she could only fight the change for so long.

"Wren!" she gasped from behind us.

"I know, baby, I know." Wren's voice was smooth and calm, which seemed to help Natalie focus on it. "Just a little longer, okay? I need you to hold on a little longer."

"I'm trying, love. I'm trying."

"We're almost there," I added, "maybe ten minutes out." I pointed to a set of traffic lights. "Turn left up here."

Natalie went silent and I glanced back at her. She was sitting in the middle seat, her eyes closed, focusing on her breathing. Meditation to control the shift. Something my father certainly hadn't taught his wolves. I wondered again just how different this new pack would be.

"Why did you help Heather with her curse?" I asked suddenly, unable to keep quiet while I was so worked up. I wanted to know more about my mate, even if it meant asking her Alpha. "I mean, most Alphas wouldn't be bothered."

Wren gave me a withering look. "Because she is my wolf. She came with a bunch of other wolves to wreak havoc in my territory. Later, she did penance and joined my pack. That made her curse my problem, and we worked together to fix it." I watched her eyes flick to the mirror as if checking on her mate. "*All* of us did."

"But she's still wounded from the curse, isn't she?"

"Too much so. She doesn't trust her wolf. She's too busy worrying that she's going to hurt someone, that she'll be what she considers a monster, to trust that her wolf knows what she's doing. That keeps a barrier between them."

"How could you let her come into the city with the full moon, knowing she can't communicate with her wolf?"

She shook her head. "I didn't want her to. I tried to talk her out of it, but I wasn't going to forbid her from seeing her mother in the hospital. If it was Heather's last chance to get some sort of closure, she deserved to have a chance at it."

"Why not come with her?"

She glanced back at Natalie again. "I have to take care of my mate too. I can't be in two places at once. I trusted her to do the right thing and hoped that things would go well."

I snorted. "Well, clearly they didn't."

"Your pack and your father certainly didn't help."

I opened my mouth to defend my pack, but realized there was no way to defend what my father had ordered or what might be happening to Heather now. "No, no we—they— certainly didn't. Especially after they found out she was my mate."

"Yeah, explain to me how that happened."

I shrugged. "The moment I scented her, I knew. My wolf

knew. We were sure that she was the one we belonged with. Then we had the dream, and I promised I'd take it slow, but when we woke up, we were already bonded."

She raised an eyebrow. "Your wolves really took care of the mate bite?"

"Yes," I said, as I rubbed at the still-healing scabs on my collarbone. The scar would never fade completely, despite us being wolves. It was a mark that would last forever. "I didn't know they could do such a thing. Yet one more thing that's not talked about in werewolf culture."

"Yeah, I'm finding there's a lot of that going around." Again, her eyes flickered back to Natalie, who was making small whimpers. "I almost missed out on the love of my life because of it."

"What happened?"

"I was told that humans couldn't handle the mate bite. That I couldn't have her."

"But you turned her."

"Because I had to. She was dying in front of me. I couldn't let her go."

"You didn't just…talk about it all?"

It was hard to tell in the glow of the streetlights, but I swore Wren's cheeks went a little red.

"I'm not…great with communication, sometimes."

I got the sense that if I pushed her further, she'd stonewall me, but I made a mental note to get the full story when things weren't quite so dire.

We made a few more turns, heading for the east end of the city where I knew this grocery store was. My father had plans for the land, to build a community center of sorts on it where his wolves could gather without worrying about prying eyes. It wasn't a terrible idea, but while the idea had taken shape, they were still working on the reality of it. So the building sat alone, untouched, and used only for bullshit like this when the Alpha needed something done quietly without the rest of the pack knowing.

I wondered how everyone else would react if they knew what he was trying to do tonight.

"For the record, everything my father is doing, I don't agree with it."

Wren glanced my way. "I never thought you did. Obviously, since you called me and had that fight with the Alpha and everything."

"I...I've been trying to get him to change. To see that he didn't need to have the pack be what it was. But he never listened."

"People in power rarely do. They know one way of doing things and can't change when presented with new options. And they don't want to risk losing their power. I try to be better than that, but I'm still going to make mistakes."

"At least your wolves aren't afraid to point out those mistakes to you."

She smiled. "Most of the time, anyway."

I pointed out the store. "That's it. Pull into the parking lot."

She did as I asked. "What are we looking at here? How many wolves are we going to have to go through for this?"

"If it's just Sinclair and his cronies, five or six. Sinclair is our Enforcer, though, so he's no pushover."

Natalie groaned in the back seat. Wren was quick to shut off the engine and let her mate out of the Jeep. The moment Natalie's feet hit the ground she was doubled over, shrugging out of her sundress and shifting into a wolf with midnight black fur and gray eyes. She circled around Wren several times, tongue lolling out and licking her mate's hand as Wren petted her.

Wren turned to me. "Front doors?"

"Let's make an entrance."

The front doors were padlocked and boarded up, but that didn't stop Wren. She reared back and knocked them in with a solid kick, her hair growing long into a mane around her head and fur rippling up her arms as she partially shifted. I joined her, feeling the strength of the shift flow through me. Natalie was a dark shadow behind us as we stormed the building to surprised yells and curses.

A wolf dashed forward, and I swiped at him with my claws, scoring a slash across his flank. He whined and disappeared behind a pile of old shelving. Wren hefted a wolf bodily and tossed them down the long disused aisle as we worked our way deeper into the store. A snarl behind me had me spinning, but dark-furred Natalie was there, lunging at another wolf who'd tried to come from behind. I had to approve of their skills. Silent and potentially deadly, they were smart enough not to cause too much trouble by killing the enemy wolves. It would only cause more trouble with the Raines pack in the long run.

"Sinclair!" I roared. "Where is she?"

"Valerie!" Sinclair's voice came from the far end of the market. "Get out of here! We're doing this for your own good."

"I swear the next person who tells me something is for my own good, I'm going to rip their throat out," I mumbled.

Wren chuckled beside me. It made me happy to have someone beside me for this. I would be here anyway, but having someone as strong as Wren beside me made all the difference when it came to cowing the wolves facing us.

After the first couple of attacks the wolves seemed to back off, like they were afraid of us. And they should be.

"Where is she?" I called out again as we neared the double doors that led to the back-warehouse area.

As we approached, the doors swung open and Sinclair himself came out to meet us, flanked by the rest of his wolves. I noted one of his usual posse missing, but there were a dozen more that he had recruited for this. He must have been expecting trouble.

"Walk away, Valerie. I'm under orders to see this done." His voice didn't have the haughtiness that it usually did. His gaze moved back and forth between Wren and me, as if he couldn't decide which of us was the more dangerous. "You're outnumbered. This is going to happen whether you like it or not."

"This is my life you're fucking with!" I snarled. "Give me Heather, and you might all live to see another day."

"You'd attack your own pack for a mutt like her?"

"I would. She's my mate!"

He looked around at his wolves. "Don't let them through."

"Sinclair, think this through. Don't sacrifice your wolves for nothing," I warned him.

He shook his head, almost sadly. "We have a job to do." He disappeared back through the doors as the wolves spread out. Some of them were in human form still, some in wolf form, but all of them looked about ready to attack. If it were only the few of his usual crew, I wouldn't have broken a sweat. But a dozen wolves, some of them I didn't know? I couldn't be sure how this was going to turn out.

I didn't have a chance to think more about it as one of the wolves lunged forward, trying to take me out at the knees. I kicked them away and ducked under another's attempted ambush. Wren laughed as she caught a partially shifted wolf by the arm and wrenched the damned thing loudly enough that it popped from its socket, and he fell to his knees with a scream. A punch followed that sent him unconscious to the ground.

"Go!" Wren called to me as Natalie played interference with a wolf that tried to pounce on Wren's back. "Get Heather, make sure she's okay!"

"What about you?"

She grinned. "I'm having fun!"

I shook my head but couldn't help but grin with her as I headed for the doors. I kicked at another wolf before he could sink teeth into me, but their attacks against me seemed half-hearted at best. They went at Wren with all the strength they possessed, but something was stopping them from trying to hurt me. Guess sometimes it pays to be the Alpha's child.

I ignored the rest and burst through the doors. In the distance was a soft murmuring sound and a louder whimpering. I headed straight for the noise, but was stopped when something grabbed my arm.

"Don't do this, Valerie," Sinclair snarled in my ear. "If you know what's good for you, you'll walk away."

I shrugged him off and continued forward. "Fuck off. I promised to protect my mate from anyone, and that includes you. Dick."

Large, furred arms wrapped around me in a tight bear hug. "I'm not going to give you another warning. I promised your father you wouldn't be hurt, but I will accomplish my mission."

I threw my head back and smashed his nose into his face. He howled and dropped me, and I rolled to my feet, heading for the chanting and whimpering again. I needed to get to her before they finished whatever was happening. I had to save her. I had to help her.

I found her on the floor, curled into the fetal position as a man in a trench coat stood over her, one hand stretched out toward her while the other raised a long-bladed knife. I didn't stop to think about it. I ran forward, howling as I threw myself into a tackle.

"No!"

CHAPTER TWENTY-ONE

Heather

The pain was so intense, it rolled through my body like wildfire, burning everything it came into contact with. It was all I could do to curl up and whimper, my throat raw and torn from screaming. Every time I opened my eyes, I caught the barest glimpse of the man in the overcoat, standing over me with a glittering knife. I'd tried to kick out at him when things first started, but the pain was too much, and now I couldn't put my thoughts together enough to fight back.

"No!"

I blinked as the pain wavered like it was a living thing and the word that echoed through the warehouse had startled it. A second later there was a howl, wordless but full of rage, and the pain disappeared altogether. It was like a cool ocean wave rolled over my body and doused the flames that Ritten's magic had left behind. I managed to uncurl my body, sore and weary but whole, and glanced around.

"V!" I croaked out. I licked my cracked and bloody lips.

V had their arms around Ritten's waist and had taken him in a hard tackle that had thrown them both to the floor. I could only watch as they struggled with each other for a moment before V got the upper hand. They closed their fingers around the hilt of the knife, and they were quick to thrust the blade against the witch's throat. Ritten went still with his eyes wide.

"Whoa!" he cried out. "What's with the hostility?"

"Don't you ever fucking touch my mate!" V roared in his face. I could see their grip on the knife almost shaking, as if warring between finishing the witch off or letting him live.

"V!" I managed again, and drew their attention. They glanced at me with those eyes that I'd grown to love.

That moment of inattention was what Ritten needed. He pushed at V with his hands and a flash of light separated them, sending V flying across the warehouse. I had to shield my eyes from the brightness, and when I looked back, Ritten was gone, the silver knife clattering to the ground where he'd been.

V pulled themselves out of a pile of forgotten boxes and refuse. They looked around as if expecting to see Ritten in front of them. They brushed themselves off and their eyes fell on me. But before they could reach me, hands grabbed my head and bodily lifted me to my feet. The hands stayed around my head, one sitting under my chin and the other at the back, like they were getting ready to twist. I struggled against the grip, but I was too worn out from everything to do more than flop around like a fish on a hook.

I reached out for my wolf, but it was like putting my hand into a pond of molasses. Everything seemed to move in slow motion, and by the time I had my wolf's attention, V was stopping a few feet in front of us, their fangs bared.

"Drop her, Sinclair."

"You've ruined everything, you spoiled little princess!" Sinclair's voice came from just over my head. "You couldn't leave it alone, could you? You were supposed to be mine. Our son would be the next Alpha!"

"Get your fucking paws off my mate."

"You only care about yourself. Not the pack, not your father. You're the only one that matters to you, aren't you?"

"What are you talking about?"

"Your father promised you to me, Valerie. We were to be mated tonight. I know he told you that!"

"Stop calling me that! My name is V! And my father has no right to give me away. We live in the twenty-first century, and I'm not going to allow myself to be part of a...a...an arranged marriage!"

"Everything you do is an affront to the pack! You're willing to destroy the future of the pack, to kill your own packmates for this bitch? Someone who doesn't matter, who isn't even a real wolf? Someone so submissive that she isn't a blip on any dominant's radar?"

"Enough with the submissive and dominant crap! It's all bullshit and you damned well know it!"

"It's the way we live our lives!"

"And it's been shown that wolves in the wild don't truly live that way. So why can't we change the way we live?"

"Because this is how our packs stay strong! Any pack that doesn't work this way is only asking to get destroyed by another!"

As if that was a cue, a new figure stepped from the shadows. My heart leaped into my throat to see Wren, fur rippling up her arms, as she pulled away the torn remnants of her shirt and wiped some blood off her chest with it. Behind her was the dark shadow of a wolf, her mouth too dripping with blood. Sinclair's grip on my head tightened and I let out a whimper.

"Anyone who lays a hand on one of my pack members is asking to be destroyed by me," Wren said, her voice more than enough of a warning. I felt Sinclair tense up even more.

"Who the fuck are you? Where are my wolves?"

She gestured behind her. "They're back there." She rubbed her shoulder, rolling it a couple times as if stretching it out. "Most of them are still alive."

"You bitch!" His hands tightened and I cried out again.

"Heather!" V screamed. "Sinclair, let her go!"

"No! I'm going to finish this!"

"Kill her and you kill me too."

"Maybe, maybe not. You know it doesn't always work that way."

"And if I die? What would you tell my father?"

He growled. "That I got the job done."

I cried out as his grip tightened a little more before a voice echoed through the warehouse.

"Enough. Let the girl go."

Like magic Sinclair's hands abruptly released me and I fell to the ground with a thud. Sinclair backed away from my flailing hands, as if I had a disease that he didn't want to risk catching. Then V was on their knees in front of me, their hands soft against my skin.

"V," I whispered into their skin as they pressed their cheek against mine, holding me close. "I knew you'd come."

"I will always be here for you."

I glanced over their shoulder. Besides Wren and Natalie, two more people had shown up. I recognized the Raines Alpha and his Lupa and turned away from them, digging my face into V's shoulder. I didn't want to deal with them or this situation. Not now. Not ever. I just wanted to get out of here.

Terra stopped a few feet away from us, wringing her hands. "I'm sorry, V. I brought him as quickly as I could. This had to stop."

I didn't feel V acknowledge their mother, but their arms tightened around me like I was a lifeline.

"Alpha." Sinclair's deep voice bounced around the warehouse. "I had things under control."

"I said enough," Desmond replied. "It's over. Stand down."

"But I—"

"I said stand down."

Another set of hands touched my skin, and I flinched before realizing they belonged to Wren, who was trying to help me to my feet. V seemed to get the point after a few seconds and helped. Between the two of them they hoisted me up so I could get my arms over their shoulders, and they completely supported my weight. A soft-furred head rubbed itself against my thigh and I sighed. I was back with the only family that mattered.

"I…I can't shift," I whispered to them.

"It'll be okay," Wren said, "we'll figure it out. Rias will help again."

The name of our witchy friend made me recall Ritten's interest in the witch who had broken his original curse. I opened my mouth to warn them, but a stronger voice boomed out, cutting me off.

"Valerie," her father said, as we passed him. "If you leave now, you will never be welcomed back to our pack."

"Father," V said, clutching me tightly as they spoke, "go fuck yourself."

Together, we slowly limped out into the main room, where a number of wolves lay on the ground, dazed or unconscious. At least one, maybe, looked like it had taken a mortal wound, but I wasn't interested in caring. Hell, I'd killed one trying to get away. They wanted to make this about that? Then let them. We would fight to the last.

When I felt better, that is.

I reached out for my wolf, afraid of what I might find,

but that molasses feeling had weakened, and I could pull at her, feel her again. That cage she had been in seemed only temporary, and I breathed a sigh of relief. I didn't know if we could survive being trapped again for good.

As she woke up, she tried to move to the forefront of our mind and initiate the shift, but I pushed her back a little.

"Soon," I whispered to myself, "soon, my wolf." If anyone else heard me, they didn't say a thing.

I managed to pull off the shift as we left the warehouse. Not only did it make the lingering pain of the witch's spells disappear, but it was nice not to have to be completely present in the moment either. I was floating in a bit of a state of bliss, knowing that V and Wren and Natalie had come for me, to save me.

I couldn't believe the Raines had managed to get the same witch that had cursed me when I was a child. I guess if you have a reputation as the best for dealing with werewolves, people are willing to pay for the best. My mother certainly was, thinking that the curse would turn me into the model little girl that she wanted. Joke was definitely on her. Look at me now. A full-on werewolf surrounded by her pack.

Wren opened the back door for me to leap up on the seat. I expected Natalie to be right behind me, but instead V, still partially shifted, climbed in. My wolf was more than happy with the placement as Natalie leapt up onto the passenger seat and Wren climbed in on the driver's side. I vaguely heard V giving her directions to someplace safe that we could go to run. My wolf and I lay down on the seat, our head comfortable on V's lap as they petted my fur and made murmuring sounds. I tried to focus on what they were saying, but my wolf didn't care much. She was exhausted. It felt more like we could just sleep through the full moon.

We ended up off the highway outside the city where

some dense woods separated several of the acreages in the area. Wren parked the Jeep, and Natalie bounded out of the car, ready to go and run. I was slower than she was, stepping out carefully and heading straight for V's outstretched hand to nuzzle against some more. The Alpha and V shifted, and we ran into the woods to work off the full moon. I lagged a bit behind. It felt like I just didn't have the energy. V stayed by my side, their wolf bounding playfully around me, as if they had been afraid they would never get to see me again. I supposed tonight there had been a very real chance of that.

That thought stuck in my head as my wolf tried to keep up with the boundless energy of my mate. What would my mother have said if Ritten had finished his job? Would I have survived it? With the silver knife he had, I doubted it.

Stop, I told myself firmly, and suddenly V halted beside us. *Wait, not you, sorry.*

What's on your mind? Their voice sounded in my head. I'd entirely forgotten we could communicate like this.

The usual. Wondering if it would have been better for the witch to finish his job.

No. Never. I would never sacrifice you for anything, Heather. I want to be with you.

Are...are you sure? I mean, I know we haven't had a lot of time together. And there has been a lot going on.

I'm sure. We have time now. We can get to know each other. I already know enough to want to be with you. We are meant to be together, you and I.

I didn't say a thing to that. I tried to believe in their words, I really did. And actions don't lie. I had to focus on V's actions. Their actions tonight told me they were telling the truth, but there was still that part of my mind that worried. I hated that part of my mind.

I tried to let go and enjoy the running and playing. V

was rambunctious and fun to play with, always taking care not to press me too hard into frolicking with them, as if they knew exactly how I was feeling—and how exhausted I was. I suppose someone trying to tear a mate bond out of you is tiring.

Finally, as the first light of day started to brighten the world around us, V lay down beside me and we cuddled for a while until Wren and Natalie returned from their run, and together we made it back to the Jeep. Everyone dressed in their discarded clothing. I borrowed a pair of sweats and a T-shirt from the back of the Jeep where Wren always kept backup clothes, then climbed into the back with V. I closed my eyes for a second as Wren started the engine, and the next time I opened them we were at V's apartment, my mate with one foot out the door and their hand outstretched toward me.

"Are you coming?" they asked softly.

I winked at them. "If you play your cards right."

Someone groaned from the front seat. I wasn't sure if it was my Alpha or her mate.

V took my hand and pulled me out of the Jeep. "I'd invite you inside, but there's only one bedroom, and I think we might—"

Natalie was quick to interrupt them. "It's all right. We'll find a place to sleep for a few hours, then come back to pick you up."

"Sounds good," V said. They closed the door with their foot and pulled me along with them.

The moment the apartment door closed behind us, V pushed me up against the wall. They grabbed my wrists in one hand and held them above my head. They pressed their lips to mine and I moaned into them, desperate for their touch. They reached down and slid their other hand into my pants and down toward my core. I squirmed under their tight grip.

"Yes," I whispered into their lips.

"Yes what?"

"Yes, please!"

V pulled back slightly until I could see their smile. "Good girl."

They plunged their fingers into me, their thumb finding my clit and playing with it as I moaned and cried out into their lips as they kissed me and stole my breath. V released my wrists but I kept them up and out of the way as they pulled up my shirt, gaining access to my nipples. They toyed with one, then the other, as if trying to give each of them equal time.

I let out a shriek as a third finger entered me and stretched my inner walls. V pumped faster and faster. They twisted and curled their fingers inside me, seeking out the most sensitive spots that would make me come undone under their touch. The wet slap of their hand against me was loud in the darkened room, echoed only by our panting and the tight moans that I couldn't keep from slipping from my throat.

"Oh! Oh, V! I'm—" My words cut off with an unintelligible noise that came deep from my throat as my climax shattered what little control I had left. My legs buckled and the only thing holding me up was V's hand on my chest, still pressing me against the wall.

"Good girl," V murmured into my ear as I felt myself leaning against them for support. "Very good girl."

"C-can we do that again sometime?" I asked softly, the question punctuated with another groan as V carefully removed their slick fingers from me. They raised them to their mouth and began to lick them clean when I reached out, took their wrist, and pulled their fingers to me so I could have a taste. I didn't know what came over me, but from the look in V's eye, they found the idea intensely arousing.

"Of course we can, darling," they said. With a little noise

of contentment I kissed them again, then let them pull me into the bedroom. The nap in the car had been enough to let us have some fun, but as soon as my head hit the pillow beside my beautiful mate, I passed out.

The morning had passed into afternoon when I blinked open my eyes and found V lying beside me, one arm wrapped around my waist and the other tucked underneath their pillow. Their chest rose and fell with their breathing, peaceful in slumber, like last night hadn't almost become a matter of life and death for us. I felt a tear start to fall as I remembered how they had come for me.

I leaned forward and kissed them, and softly ran my fingertips over their bare shoulders. They shivered at the touch and their eyes fluttered open to look at me. A wide smile crossed their lips.

"Good morning, beautiful," they said, and I wrapped myself in their words, their tone, everything I could to keep the bad thoughts and memories away.

"Good morning, my mate," I whispered. I ran my hand down their arm to their side and onto their hip. "A very good morning, with you."

I leaned over and pressed my lips against the nape of their neck, and swirled my tongue over their warm skin. They hummed appreciatively as I breathed in the scent of them, that perfect, beautiful scent that made me want them more and more. Goosebumps erupted on their neck and arm as I breathed out against them. I traced them with my tongue, drawing figures between the bumps as I coasted my hand down their hip.

"Were you interested in something?" V asked with a softness in their tone that seemed to come out when we were alone together. I didn't waste my breath as I continued to kiss and lick down their collarbone. A breathy moan escaped them, and I caught a look at their eyes, their pupils dilated with desire.

I pulled the sheets back a little as I moved down their collarbone and caressed the soft skin of their areola with my lips. It quickly pebbled under my touch, becoming hard in my mouth, and I gently rolled it back and forth with my tongue as V began to moan. They wrapped their arms around me and pressed their face into me until I could feel their breath in my hair. I sucked harder on the captured nipple, and V let out another moan and their hand moved up, pressing my hair to the side as they placed light kisses on my head.

"Keep going!" V gasped when I let go of their nipple. I blinked at them innocently, moving back to look at their face.

"Say please."

"Please." The word came out in a low growl, like they were gritting their teeth as they said it.

I smiled and gave some attention to their other nipple, taking it into my mouth as I trailed my hands down to their thighs. They opened for me immediately and I found that V was completely nude—not that any sort of panties would have stopped me. I rolled their nipple around my tongue, then bit down lightly as I slid my fingers into them. V gasped again, wordlessly, as I worked my fingers into them the way I had done the other night, trying to find that sweet spot that would make them squirm. I released the nipple with a soft pop and kissed my way down their stomach as I put my thumb to work, finding their clit and working it until it slid out from under its hood.

"There you are." I brushed my lips against their thigh and left small bites along the skin in a meandering pathway as I continued to work and tease their clit. V's breathing was coming hot and fast now as I worked them up more and more.

Then I flicked my tongue out to take in the magnificent taste of them before I reached their clit and sucked it into my mouth. Suddenly their hand was in my hair. They gripped tightly and pulled me in deeper, and I gasped, enjoying the roughness of the movement. I shoved my tongue into them, then focused on their clitoris as I worked my fingers inside them. I found that spot that made them scream my name and pressed my fingertips to it, then rubbed ever so softly as I thrust in and out.

Then V's hand, still in my hair, pulled my head away and I lost my grip on their clit. I kept my hand going as they pulled me up to them. Their lips met mine as I continued moving my fingers in and out of them. My wrist started to hurt but there was no way I was going to stop until I had brought them the pleasure that I needed to give. I watched V's face as their eyes grew heavy-lidded. They moved their hands over my hips and skin almost restlessly as I continued my attentions, and I kept my lips on theirs. They didn't seem to mind that they could taste themselves on me, and that was fucking hot.

I slid a third finger into them while working their clit with my thumb, and I must've hit the right spot because they threw their head back and cried out wordlessly into the morning air. Their back arched high before they sagged back down to the bed, my name on their lips.

"Oh, Heather," they whispered over and over again. I drew my hand back up their body and settled it between us, where they happily took my fingers into their mouth.

"Fuck, V," I groaned, "I need you."

In a flash our positions were reversed and V was atop me. With a primal grunt that under other circumstances would have me wondering how close their wolf was to the surface, they tore the sheets away and laid me bare on the bed. They nipped their way down my chest and stomach and settled between my legs. They took no time at all to bring me to that same point where I was gasping their name and swearing over and over that nothing had ever felt this good before. They worked me like an instrument that they'd practiced for years. I touched my own breasts, playing with my nipples as they worked between my thighs.

They cupped my ass and physically lifted me onto their face. I gasped and moaned as their fingernails bit into my skin. The pain meshed with the pleasure that came from down below to create a heady mix of fog that enveloped my sometimes traitorous brain.

So much for being unlovable, huh, brain?

Another moment of encouragement from them and I praised their name to the heavens. I gasped for air as waves of pleasure rushed through me one after another after another. As the waves ebbed, V pulled themself back up and pressed a hard kiss against my mouth, and I opened wide for them. I could taste myself and loved it.

As long as V was with me, I knew I was loved.

CHAPTER TWENTY-TWO

Heather

We weren't out of bed before noon, and even that took Wren almost kicking down the door to get our asses moving. I answered the door wearing one of V's T-shirts and a pair of sweats that were at least a size too big for me.

"Good afternoon," Wren said. Both she and Natalie gave me a knowing look that made heat rush up my cheeks as I looked away. "We were waiting for you."

"We got kind of carried away."

She smiled. "Don't worry, I totally understand." She wrapped an arm around Natalie's waist as they came into the apartment. "Are you ready to go?"

I hesitated. "Your car is still at the hospital, I think."

"No problem. Natalie can drive it back."

"I can drive fine."

"I know you can, but I don't want to leave you alone while we're still in the city," Wren said, holding up a hand to stop any further argument. "I don't trust the Alpha not to try something again."

"I can take care of myself."

"I'm not arguing about this, Heather. If there's anywhere

you need to go before we leave, we can do that, but I'm not giving them another chance to try to kill you."

I wanted to argue more, but damned if she didn't have a fucking point. I was saved from saying anything by V coming out of the bathroom. They stood, rubbing a towel over their hair, still wet from the shower.

"Are you going back to the hospital today?" they asked. The softness in their eyes made me want to go to them and hold them against me until every one of my mental wounds was healed.

"No. It's pointless. Neither of them will listen to me."

"Them?" Wren echoed.

"My mother and sister. My mother hasn't been awake the couple times I've gone. But I argued enough with my sister that I don't think it would be any different if my mother were awake."

"Are you certain?" Wren asked. "Because we definitely won't be welcomed back any time soon."

I shook my head. "There's no point. I know that I deserved better than what I got from my mother. Summer and I both did, honestly." I turned to V and took their hand in mine. "It took me a while, but now I know what it's like to be loved by people who actually want me around. Who don't care so much about what I am, but instead care about who I am."

V nuzzled my hand a little. I smiled at them.

"I'm not going to let that toxicity get to me anymore. I don't need their approval. I don't need them to have a fulfilling life. My mother made her choice a long time ago, and again when I was nineteen. She doesn't deserve another chance."

V pulled me to her. "Well, they're missing out on knowing a beautiful young woman."

"Thank you, babe." The term of endearment slipped out and I glanced at their face, worried they might not like it.

"You're welcome, *babe*," they replied with a laugh and a smile.

I let out a small breath. I was still learning what was okay with them and what wasn't. It was like nothing fazed them at all. I wondered how strong someone had to be for that to be the case.

I turned back to find Wren and Natalie in their own familiar kind of closeness, Natalie's forehead pressed against Wren's lips. Their eyes were closed, and they looked so damned happy that I wanted that for myself. Then I turned and met V's eyes and realized I did have it. It was right in front of me. I wasn't going to give it up for anything. My mother, their parents, another Alpha, nothing.

I stepped back up to my mate and wrapped my arms around their waist, leaning my head against their shoulder, and taking in their strength for myself.

"So, are we all ready to go?" Wren asked, after a few minutes of everyone taking some comfort from their partner.

"Ready," Natalie said.

"Yes," I whispered against V's chest.

V hesitated. I took a step back to look at them, my heart starting to pound as my mind raced and blamed myself for whatever was making them pause. Did they not want to come with us? Was this whole thing just a mistake?

"About that," they said slowly, and I felt the stupid tears already start to form in my eyes. I wasn't about to do this without them. I needed them. They were my mate. Weren't they? "I have some things to take care of here. I won't be joining you yet."

"What are you talking about?" My voice was far shriller than I would've liked.

"Darling, I can't up and leave everything behind that easily," they said. "I have a rental lease to break and a couple of favors to call in to move my stuff to Terabend. And truthfully, I want to say good-bye to my mother. My father doesn't deserve to see me again, but my mom should know that I'm happy to be leaving. I'll only be a couple of days behind you, I promise."

"Are you going to be okay by yourself?" Wren asked, sounding uncomfortable with the idea of leaving them behind. So was I. I didn't want to think about what their parents might do to them without someone to watch their back.

"I will be. It shouldn't take more than a day. Two at most, and then I'll be with you," they said. They pressed a soft kiss to my cheek.

I kept my mouth shut. I didn't trust myself to take this rationally. Not after the morning we'd had together. Not after they'd saved my life last night.

"It'll be okay, darling." Their muscled arms wrapped around me tight, and I sagged into them, still trying to fight back the tears. "I'll be there before you know it. Then we'll have all the time in the world together, okay? I promise, I won't be long."

I wiped my eyes, still unable to look them in the face.

"I don't like it," I said wetly. "I don't like it, but I'll deal with it." I lightly slapped their chest. "But you better not be long. I won't tolerate you being more than a few days."

Two fingers touched the bottom of my chin and raised my head until I looked them in the eye. "As you wish, my mate." The kiss that came next was enough to make me want to melt into a warm little puddle and at the same time jump on top of them and ride them to the floor.

As if they were expecting exactly that to happen, Wren and Natalie made cooing noises, and I flipped them the bird as we continued our kiss. Fuck them. I'd seen them do a lot more when they first found each other, after all. It was my turn to have that kind of fun.

When we finally came up for air, I reluctantly stepped away, but couldn't make it more than a couple feet before I turned back to them.

"A couple days. And if you're going to be longer, you call, understand me?"

"Of course, darling."

I turned back to Wren and Natalie. "Let's go before I change my mind and demand to stay with them."

"Are you sure you're going to be okay if you stay in the Raines territory?" Wren looked past me to my mate.

"They won't do anything to me. I'm still their child. They don't have to like my decision, but I won't let it stop me from coming to join you. As long as I'm still welcome, that is."

I snapped my head toward Wren as if there were a possibility that my mate wouldn't be welcome in our pack.

"Of course you can. The offer stands as long as you want it. You'd be a welcome addition to our pack."

I let out a shaky breath. "A couple days," I repeated.

V nodded.

I turned to the others. "Let's go."

We shuffled out of the apartment, and I took one last look back at my mate, who winked and smiled at me before I left. I knew that image of them would have to tide me over for the three-hour ride back home and a few days after that, so I tried to hold it in my head for as long as I could. Because heaven knows, my brain tended to turn traitor on me.

And with those wonderful thoughts, we started our hours-long trip back to Terabend without my mate. By the time we arrived home, my nails were going to be bitten down to the nub.

CHAPTER TWENTY-THREE

V

I took a cab back to my parents' house. My father had said that he wouldn't welcome me back, but I didn't really give a shit about being welcomed. I was there to speak with my mother. And my bike was still there from last night, so I had to pick that up too.

It was strange not to see the door open on its own, as I headed up the walkway. Stranger still to have to knock on the door. After a few moments of waiting, I started to wonder if I was going to be let in. Then the door creaked open slowly, as if whoever was behind it was reticent to open it at all.

"V." As greetings went, it wasn't the friendliest I'd ever gotten. My mother's voice was low, as if she were trying not to be heard. Under other circumstances I might have laughed, but I didn't want my choices to bring anything down on her. That wasn't fair. "You shouldn't be here right now."

"I know, I know," I said softly. "I had to come and see you before I left. Is he taking it out on you?"

She chuckled. "He's taking it out on anyone around him." She opened the door fully, but instead of ushering me in, she stepped out onto the deck with me and closed the door firmly behind her. "He's not pleased his little plan didn't work."

"Did he really expect me to bend the knee like some indentured servant, even if his plan had succeeded last night?"

"I guess I really don't know what he's thinking anymore. He's obsessed with power, with the strength of the pack, and anything that threatens that is forbidden."

I looked away. "If I hadn't resisted..."

"Then it would only have been a matter of time before someone else did the same thing, or something else imploded." She sighed. "Your father is not as strong as he was in his youth, and truthfully, last night if your new Alpha friend had challenged him for the pack, he probably would not have won."

"The pack needs new leadership."

"True, it does, but there are fewer and fewer Alphas coming of age in our world. And those that do show up are often coveted by their packs, leaving them little reason to search out a pack of their own. We need new blood, to be honest, and a new Alpha would be ideal."

"I've never really heard of any wolf leaving their pack for another one."

She raised an eyebrow.

"I mean, except what I'm doing."

"It's because it doesn't happen often. And that is exactly why the packs run the way they normally do."

"I still don't understand why father is so adamant about the way the pack works. About furthering the myth of dominant and submissive among all of us."

She sighed again, nudging me to the side so she could take a seat in a low Adirondack chair sitting on the porch. I leaned against the railing, waiting patiently.

"We were almost wiped out, a good number of centuries ago," she began. "You might've heard about it at some point. The problem was that the packs had gotten too large. The

Alphas were stretched tight by how many pack members they bonded with, and they started to go mad. The largest packs went to war with each other. By the time the survivors stopped fighting, the hunters had come down on us and almost wiped us out."

"Holy shit. I know this story but didn't realize it was that dire."

"It was. The surviving Alphas scattered around the world, finding their own territories and building their own packs, using the dominance and submission hierarchy that you rail against. It allowed the Alphas to bond with the strongest of the pack. In that way, the Alpha kept the pack strong. But there also needed to be mates for the strong, so the Alpha would use the dominants' mate bonds to make sure the weaker wolves would stay with the pack and not leave. Because our packs still lived by *the more, the stronger*. But not too many."

"That…that is so fucked up."

She shrugged. "Maybe we're simply slow to learn our lessons. But since then, this is how the packs have been run. And they've never looked too favorably on strong women wolves either, but then that is a history we share with humans as well."

"But it doesn't have to be that way. We can change things."

She shook her head sadly. "Only an Alpha can change things, and most are indoctrinated into the way the packs are run by the time they come of age. If we could know when someone is going to be an Alpha, maybe we could do something different—but as it is now, I know your father will never change. Not enough, anyway. Never enough to make a difference for you."

I looked away from my mother. "I didn't want to leave."

"It's better for you if you do."

"What about you?"

"What about me?"

"Who's going to take care of you?"

She smacked my arm lightly. "I can take care of myself, thank you very much."

"You know what I mean, *Mother*."

"You don't need to worry about me, my dear. I'll be fine. Your father will too, given time. He needs to learn that he's not always right."

"I don't understand why he thought he could control me like that."

"Because he is the Alpha. And I think he's getting desperate. I'm not getting any younger, and I doubt we'll have another pup. So that left only you for a chance to have an Alpha in the family line."

"You know I'd be an Alpha if I could change it."

"I know, dear, I know. But that's not your role. You were our Knight, our problem solver." She sighed and got out of her chair, slower than I would have liked to see. "No, you will find your place in the world, as we all must. And you will do it as exactly who you are. And now, you can do it with your fated mate." She smiled. "I am so glad I got to meet her, even if it was under terrible circumstances. Our mates are a gift from the Mother. It's something we've long forgotten."

"More wolves should have the chance to find their mates like I did. We keep everyone so close, so afraid they might go to another pack, or something. It's...claustrophobic."

"That's a good word for it," she admitted. "It is claustrophobic. But that united front is what kept us alive. It would be hard to change it all, even if we weren't capable of living for a couple centuries." She patted me on the arm again. "But it is no longer your problem, is it? You should go and join with your new pack, find your new role. I'm sure your mate misses you."

My blush came fast and furious, but I ran with it. "I'm sure she does too, but I couldn't leave without saying good-bye. To you, at the very least."

"And I appreciate it." She stood and headed back toward the door. I followed a step behind her. "I have something for you, if you have the time to wait," she said over her shoulder.

"I do."

"Good," she said, and opened the door, "but if I were you I would wait outside."

I let her go. I didn't want to risk Father's wrath falling on her should she be found to allow me inside. Which felt ridiculous. To be afraid that your father would hurt your mother because of you? What was happening to my family?

If I hadn't mated with Heather, if I hadn't started all of this, then I wouldn't have to worry about my mother or my family. But I couldn't live my life solely based on what they wanted. No child should be forced to live their life solely to meet their parents' expectations. I had to believe that my mother could take care of herself. And if she couldn't, well, maybe my new pack would have to intervene.

"Excuse me." I spun around as someone cleared their throat behind me. A young man stood on the walkway, a few feet from the steps to the porch. He looked vaguely familiar but didn't seem to be hostile toward me. "You, you go by V, right?"

"That's me." I moved to block the stairs in case things turned ugly. Something in my memory clicked and I recognized the kid. He was the one who had fought Sinclair only a couple nights ago. So much had happened since then, it felt like a long time ago. "Cale, right?"

"You remember me?"

"I try to remember everyone I help. It keeps me going." I came down the steps and offered him my hand. "I'm glad to see you recovering from the fight with Sinclair. How can I help you? In case you hadn't heard, I'm not a member of this pack anymore."

He took my hand timidly, but there was strength behind his grip. I would've bet that he could be a strong dominant wolf in the pack, if given the chance, but that would be hard to break into here. The only way to do that would be fighting other wolves, and without a lot of training and a bloodlust I didn't think he possessed, that would be hard for him. He was a protector, not a savage.

"That's, um, why I'm here. Why I wanted to talk to you. Why we"—he gestured behind himself—"wanted to talk to you."

I glanced over his shoulder and noticed several more of the pack's younger members congregating on the sidewalk, near my bike. I thought I recognized the two women who had helped Cale leave the parking garage the other night, but I couldn't be sure.

"When are you, I mean, you're leaving, right?"

"I was hoping to leave in the morning. I need to find a moving truck and maybe call in some favors from people willing to help." I gestured to the door behind me. "And I wanted to say good-bye to my mom."

"I get that," he said, but didn't make eye contact with me. Again I was reminded how young he was. Barely out of his teens, probably, and not confident in his place. I couldn't say I blamed him. Being told you're submissive time and time again when you're not can mess with a wolf. It was why I had worked so hard to be considered dominant. Why I had fought my way to my title as Knight.

"Well, we were wondering if maybe, um…" He trailed off and looked over his shoulder, as if for inspiration.

I opened my mouth to ask what he wanted when the door

opened behind me. Cale jumped a little and looked about to run for his life but managed to stand his ground. He rose higher in my estimation for that.

"V." My mother's voice was soft behind me. "I have this for you."

She hefted a heavy duffel bag out the door with her and set it on the porch beside me. I glanced down at it, wondering exactly what she could possibly be giving me.

"Mother, what—"

She shook her head. "Don't, V. Just take it, okay? It's yours anyway, it just took me a while to get it to you."

She looked between me and Cale.

"And make time for this boy. You can help him. You can help all of them."

"What?" I asked, but she was already heading back inside. "Mother, what are you talking about?"

She smiled before the door closed. "I love you, V. Go find your new role."

I didn't get a chance to ask anything else as the door closed and I heard the locks click closed. Added security to put between my father and me? Possibly. I kneeled down and unzipped the bag to take a little peek inside.

Fabric. Fabric wrapped around what looked like a few rectangular bundles. Money. She'd given me money. I wasn't going to be crass and start counting it in front of Cale and his friends, but there were at least several thousand dollars there, if not more.

"Damn it, Mother," I muttered under my breath. I hefted the bag and came down the steps closer to Cale, who still looked like he was ready to run away.

"So what can I do for you and your friends, Cale?" I wrapped my other arm around his shoulders and pulled him along with me as I headed for my bike.

"We want you to take us with you."

"What do you mean?"

"To your new pack. We want to go with you."

I looked over him and the group that we soon caught up to. There were only about half a dozen more wolves in the group, mostly women who were considered submissive, but a couple of young men too.

"Why? Why risk going to a new pack when you're already part of this one?"

Cale shook his head. "You've seen the way they treat us. The so-called *dominants*. We're all tired of it." He looked around at his group and seemed to draw strength from their proximity. "You helped me at the fight. Made sure Sinclair didn't kill me. I know we weren't very polite to you that night, but you seemed honest in wanting to help more. And this... this is our chance for something new. Same as you."

"Why not reach out to a different Alpha yourselves?"

"Because if the packs are anything like this one, they won't give us the time of day. Maybe they'll accept our membership, but nothing will change. We still won't have a place in the pack until a dominant decides they want one of us for a mate."

There was a general murmur of consensus from the small crowd.

"How do you know my new pack will be any different?"

He let out a small chuckle. "Word gets around, V. We know about what happened at the grocery store last night. How you and the other Alpha stood up to Sinclair and our Alpha. And you might not realize it, but we've been watching you."

"Watching me?"

He flinched. "Oh that sounds bad, doesn't it? That's not what I mean. We know you want to change things. I've seen it. We've all heard that you fight with the Alpha all the time. I don't think you'd go to a new pack that didn't accept you, that wasn't different than what we already have."

I sighed and wondered how mad at me Wren would be if I showed up with an entourage. "How many are you?"

Cale looked around. "A few more than what you see here. We've been careful about who we talk to. We don't want the dominants to know what's going on."

"Fuck." I hadn't considered what might happen if these pups got caught pulling this stunt. I pulled out my phone. "How soon can you be ready?" I asked.

He looked behind him again at the small crowd. "Most of us can be ready today. We don't have a lot. We live in the houses the pack has for submissives—you know the ones."

I did. There were small houses near to the pack's Alpha where those who didn't make a living wage could stay. It was one of the few adjustments to pack life I'd talked my father into implementing. Of course, that meant the submissives were shunted into those homes while the dominants in the pack were given stipends to afford their own places. The wolves that lived in those places were only allowed a large duffel of personal items.

"I do." I took a deep breath and hoped Wren wasn't going to kill me for this. "If you can be ready by tomorrow morning, you can join me for the ride in. Find something, a van or a bus, to drive everyone there, and make sure there's nothing left behind that you need. Because odds are good you won't be welcomed back." I looked him square in the eyes, then let my gaze fall on each and every one of the wolves assembled behind him. "Do you have someone who can drive a U-Haul?" I asked.

"I can," Cale said.

"Good, you can help me. We'll load up with everyone's stuff and leave early tomorrow." I looked him dead in the eye again and raised my voice a little to address all the wolves surrounding us. "And I promise nothing about being allowed into the new pack. I am not the Alpha. She is reasonable, but I will abide by her decision. Do you understand?"

There was a rumbling murmur of agreement from the crowd.

"All we want is the chance. For a new life," Cale said, a little too enthusiastically.

"It'll be that," I muttered. I traded phone numbers with him, then settled the duffel bag across my back. I climbed on my bike and started the engine. "Get your wolves together. I'll text you my address," I said.

Cale turned back to his wolves. His pack. He seemed like more of a leader already than my father had been this last while. It would be interesting to see him grow more in a new environment.

I pulled out and hit the street, opening up the throttle and heading back to my apartment. I had to figure out what to do with all my crap before I left for Terabend. Now with a half dozen or more wolves at my back too.

I hoped that Wren wouldn't be too angry with me. I wasn't only bringing her a strong wolf in me, but now a whole damned pack of youngsters.

CHAPTER TWENTY-FOUR

Heather

I'd been in difficult spots before. Homeless for a while, and after that, on the lowest rung of a pack's ladder. I'd had my wolf locked up for years and gone through a painful transformation that first night when I transformed. And yet through everything, nothing was as bad as waiting for my mate. I missed them. Missed them more than anything.

I threw myself back into work. I'd taken a job at the diner six months ago after the usual front-end girl had quit after a dustup with some werewolves. Now she was happily making and selling art from her home. My job wasn't difficult, and getting to know the people of the town was kind of a fun game in itself. At least it usually kept me occupied during the duller times at the diner. But not now. Now every customer that came in was one more reminder that V wasn't here with me. That I had to wait and hope that they would show up. Something I couldn't say I was good at.

Outside of work I was trying to improve my connection to my wolf. It was coming along, I thought, though it still felt like she didn't entirely trust me not to push her away again. I didn't plan to. We meditated together, and I worked on shifting at will. That last night of the full moon, I gave her the reins and let her run free in the woods with Wren and Natalie. It had been the freest I'd ever felt in my life. I wanted to share it with V.

It was early afternoon the day after we left the city and I was at work once more, idly wiping down the clean bar with a clean rag when someone sat down right across from me. I looked up to find my friend Rias watching me closely, a thin smile on her lips.

I realized I'd been staring at her for a long minute when her smile widened. "So I hear someone has a mate now. When do we get to meet them?"

I glanced around. There was no one really nearby—the diner was nearly empty and the cooks in the back were listening to music rather loudly. I was safe to tell her everything. And I did. Slowly but surely, she coaxed the entire story out of me, from going back to the city, to meeting with my sister, and to finding my mate.

"And now I'm waiting, impatiently, for them to arrive here. Because they said they would, and Wren said they'd have a spot in the pack." And there was a part of me that was still worried about whether or not they could stay, knowing that ultimately the decision would be up to Vadi, the Genius Loci. I hadn't seen Vadi since the night of the engagement party, but I knew that they would be aware of my return and V's arrival.

Rias smiled. "Don't worry, they'll be here sooner than you think."

"What, you psychic or something?"

"No, but I am a witch."

"Clearly," I said. I smiled at her. It was thanks to Rias that I had my wolf back. She'd helped break the curse last summer. I owed her so much more than I ever thought I could repay.

"I just miss them, you know? Even though it's only been a day or so." I sighed and rested my arms on the counter. "And

I'm afraid. I'm scared that because we're apart they'll change their mind and decide not to come after all. That I'm not good enough to make the trip for."

"Well, they would be a fool not to come and be with their mate, especially if wolf mating works the way I believe it to. They'll be missing you just as much. Can't you feel that inside you?"

I felt a blush and turned away from the intensity of their gaze. "I'm having trouble figuring out what is theirs and what is mine, to be honest. I'm not great at recognizing my own emotions most of the time, and it just gets confusing adding in a whole other person's." I sighed and shook my head. "The problem is that they could do so much better than me. They didn't need to settle for someone so broken, someone who can't regulate their emotions or will push them away at the first sign of anything going wrong. I'm that kind of person, the kind that drives people away and—"

"And how is that working for you now that you have a proper family?"

"What?"

"It seems that Wren and Natalie have no intention of being driven away by you. And I am certain that your mate feels that very same way."

"But I—"

Rias shook her head. "No buts. You've built a family around you, Heather. The pack, this diner, the town. You're good at your job and like to joke with people, even if it's a little self-deprecating at times. People love you—you only have to be willing to let them."

"I don't know if I know how to do that."

"There is no time like the present to learn."

I took a deep breath without really looking at them, afraid they'd see the lie in my eyes. It wasn't that I didn't want to listen or didn't want to do it. It was that I wasn't sure if I could. I didn't have any idea how to make it happen, how to let people in like that. I'd trusted Wren because I'd needed her help, and Natalie because they were a package deal. I'd trusted V, after they stood between their pack and me. At least I tried to. But was I willing to let these people in further? Or would I be lonely for the rest of my long, long life?

I shivered at the idea.

"I'm sorry," I said. I pulled out my notepad and pencil. I had only worked here six months and I wasn't good at memorizing orders yet. "I haven't asked what I can get you—"

The pencil fell from my hands when I heard the familiar roar of a motorcycle engine. Ignoring everything else, I ran around the counter and was out the door before anyone could stop me.

A familiar motorcycle pulled in off the highway into the parking lot, and a beautiful enby in a leather jacket steered it into a spot right by the front door. They were barely off the bike before I threw myself at them. They spun and caught me, and wrapped one arm around my waist while pulling their helmet off with the other hand.

"You're here! You're really here."

"Of course I am," V said as they wrapped their other arm around me. They pressed their lips against mine and I took their face in my hands, never wanting to let go. They pulled back and adjusted their grip and I wrapped my legs around their waist. "Did you doubt me?"

"Not for a second."

They smiled. "Yeah, right."

I felt the heat creep up my face as I was caught in my lie. I glanced at the bike, then back at V. I noticed they only had a small duffel bag slung on their back. "Where's all your things?"

They hesitated for a second too long, and I unwrapped my legs and let them put me down.

"Yeah," they began, "about that."

Any more words were drowned out by a school bus that rumbled into the parking lot of the diner and came to a stop by the sign where no one usually parked. I'd seen passenger busses come and go a couple times in my tenure at the diner, but never a school bus. And especially not one that smelled suspiciously like wolves.

"What's going on?"

"I think I need to talk to Wren about this." V's voice was soft and worried. Whatever was happening, would it change Wren's mind about letting V into the pack? I glanced from the school bus back to my mate. No. I wouldn't let it happen. I didn't care what was going on, V was going to be welcomed here. They had to be.

"I'll go get her." I started to turn to head back in, but V grabbed my arm and pulled me back. V's lips were on mine again and I melted into the kiss. Their tongue pressed for permission, and I opened for them, letting them take as much of me as I could give. I trusted them. I needed them. Whatever was going on, it was going to be okay.

I had to believe it.

Their tongue grazed mine as our lips parted, and left a slickness on my lower lip that made me want to bite it and keep the taste in my mouth forever. I looked up into their eyes and found them staring back at me with a yearning need that I felt strongly in my gut.

"V." Wren's voice behind me was one of the only things that stopped me from jumping their bones right in the middle of the parking lot. "What's going on?"

I turned around and saw Wren and Natalie walking side by side out of the diner. They took in V and the school bus that had thrown open its doors, and the several people who started to slowly disembark. I was right in my assessment that they were wolves, but none that smelled overly familiar—except one.

"Trish?" I whispered, my hackles rising at the scent of the nurse who had led me to Sinclair. "What is she doing here?"

"Settle, darling. It's okay. She's here for a new life," V said softly, then turned to Wren as she walked up to us. "These wolves want a new life, with a new pack. A pack that doesn't follow the old ways, that doesn't abuse or leave weaker wolves in the dirt while holding up the strongest to be the pinnacle of our society. They need a new home, like I do."

A moment later a small U-Haul parked in behind the bus and another wolf came out to join those who'd come off the bus. They crowded around him until he was pushed to the front, like he was their spokesperson or something.

Wren looked over V, then at the wolves that were still coming off the bus. Ten, twelve, fourteen wolves in total were standing behind the young man, who carefully looked at Wren without challenge. Most of them carried a bag or two which was probably all their important worldly possessions. I knew from experience that the lowest in the pack were often given beds in what amounted to group homes, leaving little space for personal items.

"V...I don't know," Wren said softly, looking over the line of wolves again, "I've never wanted a pack. I don't see myself as anyone's Alpha. What if it doesn't work? What if they want more than I can do, than I can give?"

Natalie took Wren's face in her hands and forced the Alpha to look at her. "You'll be exactly who you are. Nothing more and nothing less. If they don't like it, they don't need to be here."

Wren let out a long sigh, then stood a little straighter and turned back to V. She held out her hand. V took it gratefully.

"Welcome to Terabend."

With cheers in the background from the collected wolves, I leapt into V's arms again. They swung me around and planted kisses on my lips until my head was full of heady thoughts.

"My mate," I whispered against their mouth.

"I'm here," they said softly. "I'm home."

Home. That had a good ring to it. Nowhere had felt like home until now. Wherever V was, that would be home to me now.

"It's good to be home."

EPILOGUE

Heather

The next month passed quietly. It was a struggle at first, dealing with newcomers to the pack when none of us knew what the hell we were doing. An Alpha who didn't want a pack, a Lupa who had only recently been turned into a werewolf, a shifter still learning to communicate with her wolf, and an ex-Knight from a very different pack. We were a motley crew working together to make sure we had a pack we could be proud of. At first the young man, Cale, had been nominated something of a spokesperson for the rest of the pack, and all of the issues or requests came to us through him. But over time they opened up to the rest of us, and so far, things were gelling pretty good.

As much as it had been a terrible idea to go and see my birth family, I couldn't say I totally regretted it. If I hadn't done it, I might never have found my mate, or even if I had found them, it might've been too late for us to be together. And I had learned to communicate with my wolf, something I was still working on. It wasn't perfect, but we worked together now instead of against one another. We learned and taught each other, and I was close to feeling confident that I'd have the same kind of connection that other wolves my age had, soon enough. V was always patient with me, and with their help I felt I was really coming into my own.

As I came down the stairs of the house that we had purchased together with the money from Terra, I heard voices from the kitchen. I pulled my hair back into a loose ponytail and made sure I was decent before I descended the rest of the way and found Wren and Natalie sitting at the table, speaking with V. They were laughing and joking, and it warmed my heart to see my mate being included and wanted.

"Heather," V said and stood from their seat to come around and wrap their arms around me.

"Hi, babe." I nuzzled into them for a moment, ignoring the catcalls from Wren and Natalie. "What's going on?"

"We were about to head to the bar and see how everything's shaping up. Did you want to come?"

"Yes!"

The bar was a labor of love for Wren and V. Partnered together, and with V's money, the two of them had decided to build a new bar in the empty lot beside the diner. They figured they'd get a good crowd being on the highway, and it was a good way to keep some of the new pack members employed. At this point most of them were sharing shifts with each other at the diner or filling in wherever they could in the town. Each and every one of them wanted to do something worthwhile, or at least helpful—things they never got the chance to do in their old pack.

The building itself was almost done. The inside still needed furnishing and the small kitchen that was going in the back room still needed appliances, but the floors and walls were finished. They planned to serve a very small menu to the patrons at the bar, mostly because the Tooth and Claw Diner was right across the lot. Some of the new wolves loitered around the place and were helping clean it up in preparation for the rest of the renovations. They waved as we entered and went about their duties, and we tried not to bother them too much.

It was amazing to see something coming together with all of us working on it. The new wolves were helping to build a place that we could all call home. Wren and V moved around the space, and Natalie and I sat at a small table with the floor plan for the bar. Booths and tables would be added in the next week, and we had purchased a couple of billiard tables for the rear area. I noticed someone had already hung an inclusive pride flag on the wall behind the bar, and I couldn't help but smile. How many of these wolves had we saved from a life of denying who they really were? How many could now be open about who they were or who they hoped to be?

"She needed this," Natalie said suddenly.

"What?" I turned to look at her, not sure I'd heard her right. "Who?"

"Wren. She needed this." She gestured toward her mate, who was talking with a couple of the wolves who'd been helping out. They laughed and she gave one a pat on the shoulder, and he beamed. "It's brought her out of her shell, more than I was able to by myself."

"I'm glad to hear that." And I was. The Alpha who never wanted a pack at all seemed like a natural leader for all the new pups.

"How's V settling in?"

"They're happy here. I think they feel like they can really grow here, not like with their old pack. I think it helped that they had the other wolves come with them too. Gave them a bit more of a sense of family." I smiled at her. "Not that the three of us wouldn't have been enough, but it's different, you know?"

"I get what you mean. It was like when I first came here. Everyone around me made it friendly. Made us a family. Now it's just a little bit bigger."

It certainly was. By a dozen or so wolves. But as I opened my mouth to say something, the large window at the front of the bar shattered as something large rocketed through the glass. Wren and V immediately moved to protect the wolves near them as Natalie and I backed up. I stared at the large cinderblock sitting on the floor, then out through the broken window. A small group of people stood outside the bar, standing in front of a large black truck and a few other vehicles.

"Valerie!" An all-too-familiar voice hollered from outside the diner. "Get your ass out here!"

I glanced toward V, but their eyes were on Sinclair in the parking lot. I couldn't believe the brute of a man would come all the way here and do something like this. Or that V's father might have sent him. Somehow that seemed worse.

"Stay here," Wren said loudly enough to include everyone in the bar.

"He wants me," V replied.

"No!" I shouted and drew V's attention to me. "I'm not going to stand by and let him hurt you."

V moved around the shattered glass and wrapped me up in their arms. The hug was quick and not nearly as reassuring as I needed, but their voice was confident when they spoke. "It's you I'm worried about. He can't hurt me as long as you're okay."

"Okay. Give him hell."

Wren headed for the door, V on her trail. They shared a glance and then Wren opened the door for them and they both left the building. Natalie was quick in assessing the damage. She handed out brooms to the wolves standing around. She didn't bother handing one to me as I made my way to the window to watch whatever was about to happen. She knew I was too focused on V to be of any use.

Several trucks had rumbled up into the parking lot without us realizing it. The entire place stank of macho wolf bullshit. Or at least that was the smell of Sinclair and his Raines pack cronies, who had formed a loose semicircle around the entrance to the bar.

"You are in another Alpha's territory." Wren's voice rang out over the half dozen newcomers. "And your first act is one of disrespect?"

"You kidnapped our wolves! That's an act of aggression. Of war!" Sinclair roared.

V snorted. "No one was kidnapped. They came willingly. Begged me to bring them, in fact. Mostly to get away from you!"

Wren shot V a look that said *shut up*. I knew V was worried about stepping on their Alpha's toes too much. This was one of those times, and V quieted immediately.

"The wolves were not taken against their will," Wren said. "And you don't have the power to declare war on my pack. Only your Alpha can do that. So get in your cars and leave, and this time—and this time only—we'll forget about this little tantrum of yours."

But Sinclair's eyes weren't on Wren. Those beady little pinpoints were focused on the window. On me. I knew he wasn't going to back down, not with his posse to back him up. He couldn't be seen to be weak. It would break him beyond his recent failures. And there had been a lot of them.

I didn't expect what happened next, though.

Instead of replying, Sinclair dashed at Wren without shifting. He was quick, but Wren was quicker. She caught his fist as he tried to sucker-punch her, and held it tight, growling at him.

"This is not happening. Get in your cars and go home. This is your last chance."

She pushed him back several steps and he roared at her, fur erupting on his arms and face as he rushed at her again. This time V got in his way. They quickly pulled a partial shift before catching Sinclair's arm and spinning, throwing him into the middle of the semicircle his wolves had created.

"If I may, Alpha?" V asked. Wren narrowed her eyes but nodded anyway. V turned back to Sinclair, who was getting to his feet.

"Your father will hear about this, *Valerie!*" He spat their deadname into the sky like it was venomous.

"Like I give a shit? He lost the chance to have me as his child when he tried to have my mate killed."

With a roar Sinclair rushed forward, but V ducked under his swiping arm and hit him in the gut with their shoulder, pushing him back again. He regained his balance quickly and slashed at their face, but V slipped under him again and caught him in the leg with their claws. He howled with pain and rage, and they both backed up until they could properly face each other.

"Go home, Sinclair," V said. "Save what face you have left and go home."

He bounded forward, and again V slipped to the side and raked their claws across his abdomen before leaping back and out of his reach. He was panting now and held his side as blood trickled down his shirt.

"You fucking bitch!" he shouted. "I don't care what your father says. I'm going to fucking kill you."

I had to look away as they clashed again and again. I heard the grunts and roars, and a cheer from Sinclair's posse, then looked up in time to see V throw themselves backward out of Sinclair's reach. A trickle of blood ran from the side of their mouth. I gasped as Sinclair's claws opened several deep furrows in V's arm and blood oozed up through their fur. He was fighting with a finesse that surprised me. I had thought he was nothing more than a savage brute. I guess fighting his way up the pack to be the Enforcer had made him stronger than V had anticipated.

They traded blow after blow, some landing, some avoided, until they were both bloody and panting. I let out a scream as I saw him batter my mate down with blows that they tried to parry on their arms. V was on their back foot and Sinclair wasn't letting them find their balance.

Then V dropped back and struck out at his knee as he brought his weight down on it. He roared in pain as the leg buckled beneath him and he fell. I was ready to climb out the damned window and attack him myself before I watched V slam their fist into his nose once, twice, thrice, until it was bloody and crushed to a pulp. He tried to fight back, but V was too quick and caught him with a strong knee to the chin that put him down on the pavement for good.

I was out the window by the time V limped back to Wren. I pulled them to me and helped keep them standing at Wren's side. The Alpha eyed me sternly, but I saw the sparkle in her eye that said she was trying to remain stoic.

"Anyone else?" she called to the other wolves that had surrounded us. When none of them moved, she scoffed. "Fine. Then take him home and get him healed up. And never bother us again."

The Raines pack wolves moved silently. Two of them picked up Sinclair and got him in one of the vehicles. One by one they climbed into their vehicles until only one was left. I recognized him as one of the wolves who'd been at the grocery store that night.

"The Alpha won't be happy about this," he announced in

a clear voice. "You will never be allowed back in our territory. Any of you."

"I don't give a shit," Wren replied, "Get the hell out of my territory and tell your Alpha to start treating his wolves better or more are going to leave him."

He didn't say anything more as he climbed into the big truck and peeled out of the parking lot. He revved his truck loudly as soon as he hit the highway.

A cheer went up from within the bar, and Wren led the way back inside. V and I moved a little slower with V limping, and we hesitated at the doorway.

"I'm all bloody, you sure—" V began.

"Get your ass in here, Beta."

I stared at my Alpha. Bestowing the title of Beta on V meant that they were now second in command of the pack. If the Alpha was away or indisposed, they would make decisions for the entire pack. For a pack to have a Beta wolf wasn't common these days. It was too much like sharing power for most Alphas, but Wren wasn't like most Alphas.

V glanced down at the ground, then back up at Wren. "Thank you."

"You've earned it."

We moved back into the bar and I helped V down on one of the chairs around the table.

"Are you okay?" I asked softly, then nuzzled their cheek. "You were amazing."

"I'll be fine after I shift," they replied. "I just wanted to make sure you were okay first."

"I'm fine, but we should get you patched up."

V grinned. "I told you I'd never let him touch you again."

"You did, my love, you did." I slapped their nonwounded arm. "Now go shift and heal."

"Yes ma'am." They got up and headed for the back room.

A second later V's wolf emerged from the room and trotted over to me, sat down, and let their tongue hang out of their mouth.

I gave them some love as the other wolves cleaned up the glass and Wren got to work finding some plywood to cover the damage until it could be repaired. They all acted like attacks like this happened every day and were nothing new. I was afraid that if the Raines Alpha got involved, it might actually be something that happened every day.

But I looked around again at what we were building. Something that everyone could be proud of. Something of their own, that they would be willing to fight for.

And I'd been lucky enough to find something of my own. I had my wolf. I had my pack. I had a wonderful Alpha and her beautiful Lupa. And I had V.

I'd found a family. Where I never expected to find it, with people I never knew I'd meet. I'd found a family.

My family.

About the Author

Elena (https://writerinawarehouse.wordpress.com) is a transwoman, parent, and wife to her amazing Goddess. She plays video games, reads books, and plays D&D on both sides of the DM screen. She lives in Edmonton, Alberta, with her wonderful spouse and child, alongside the pets who think they rule the house.

Keep in touch through email at Writerprincess8@gmail.com or find her online on Twitter at @WriterElenaA or on her seldom-touched blog.

Books Available From Bold Strokes Books

Hands of the Morri by Heather K O'Malley. Discovering she is a Lost Sister and growing acquainted with her new body, Asche learns how to be a warrior and commune with the Goddess the Hands serve, the Morri. (978-1-63679-465-5)

I Know About You by Erin Kaste. With her stalker inching closer to the truth, Cary Smith is forced to face the past she's tried desperately to forget. (978-1-63679-513-3)

Mate of Her Own by Elena Abbott. When Heather McKenna finally confronts the family who cursed her, her werewolf is shocked to discover her one true mate, and that's only the beginning. (978-1-63679-481-5)

Pumpkin Spice by Tagan Shepard. For Nicki, new love is making this pumpkin spice season sweeter than expected. (978-1-63679-388-7)

Sweat Equity by Aurora Rey. When cheesemaker Sy Travino takes a job in rural Vermont and hires contractor Maddie Barrow to rehab a house she buys sight unseen, they both wind up with a lot more than they bargained for. (978-1-63679-487-7)

Taking the Plunge by Amanda Radley. When Regina Avery meets model Grace Holland—the most beautiful woman she's ever seen— she doesn't have a clue how to flirt, date, or hold on to a relationship. But Regina must take the plunge with Grace and hope she manages to swim. (978-1-63679-400-6)

We Met in a Bar by Claire Forsythe. Wealthy nightclub owner Erica turns undercover bartender on a mission to catch a thief where she meets no-strings, no-commitments Charlie, who couldn't be further from Erica's type. Right? (978-1-63679-521-8)

Western Blue by Suzie Clarke. Step back in time to this historic western filled with heroism, loyalty, friendship, and love. The odds are against this unlikely group—but never underestimate women who have nothing to lose. (978-1-63679-095-4)

Windswept by Patricia Evans. The windswept shores of the Scottish Highlands weave magic for two people convinced they'd never fall in love again. (978-1-63679-382-5)

A Calculated Risk by Cari Hunter. Detective Jo Shaw doesn't need complications, but the stabbing of a young woman brings plenty of those, and Jo will have to risk everything if she's going to make it through the case alive. (978-1-63679-477-8)

An Independent Woman by Kit Meredith. Alex and Rebecca's attraction won't stop smoldering, despite their reluctance to act on it and incompatible poly relationship styles. (978-1-63679-553-9)

Cherish by Kris Bryant. Josie and Olivia cherish the time spent together, but when the summer ends and their temporary romance melts into the real deal, reality gets complicated. (978-1-63679-567-6)

Cold Case Heat by Mary P. Burns. Sydney Hansen receives a threat in a very cold murder case that sends her to the police for help, where she finds more than justice with Detective Gale Sterling. (978-1-63679-374-0)

Proximity by Jordan Meadows. Joan really likes Ellie, but being alone with her could turn deadly unless she can keep her dangerous powers under control. (978-1-63679-476-1)

Sweet Spot by Kimberly Cooper Griffin. Pro surfer Shia Turning will have to take a chance if she wants to find the sweet spot. (978-1-63679-418-1)

The Haunting of Oak Springs by Crin Claxton. Ghosts and the past haunt the supernatural detective in a race to save the lesbians of Oak Springs farm. (978-1-63679-432-7)

Transitory by J.M. Redmann. The cops blow it off as a customer surprised by what was under the dress, but PI Micky Knight knows they're wrong—she either makes it her case or lets a murderer go free to kill again. (978-1-63679-251-4)

Unexpectedly Yours by Toni Logan. A private resort on a tropical island, a feisty old chief, and a kleptomaniac pet pig bring Suzanne and

Allie together for unexpected love. (978-1-63679-160-9)

Crush by Ana Hartnett Reichardt. Josie Sanchez worked for years for the opportunity to create her own wine label, and nothing will stand in her way. Not even Mac, the owner's annoyingly beautiful niece Josie's forced to hire as her harvest intern. (978-1-63679-330-6)

Decadence by Ronica Black, Renee Roman & Piper Jordan. You are cordially invited to Decadence, Las Vegas's most talked about invitation-only Masquerade Ball. Come for the entertainment and stay for the erotic indulgence. We guarantee it'll be a party that lives up to its name. (978-1-63679-361-0)

Gimmicks and Glamour by Lauren Melissa Ellzey. Ashly has learned to hide her Sight, but as she speeds toward high school graduation she must protect the classmates she claims to hate from an evil that no one else sees. (978-1-63679-401-3)

Heart of Stone by Sam Ledel. Princess Keeva Glantor meets Maeve, a gorgon forced to live alone thanks to a decades-old lie, and together the two women battle forces they formerly thought to be good in the hopes of leading lives they can finally call their own. (978-1-63679-407-5)

Peaches and Cream by Georgia Beers. Adley Purcell is living her dreams owning Get the Scoop ice cream shop until national dessert chain Sweet Heaven opens less than two blocks away and Adley has to compete with the far too heavenly Sabrina James. (978-1-63679-412-9)

The Only Fish in the Sea by Angie Williams. Will love overcome years of bitter rivalry for the daughters of two crab fishing families in this queer modern-day spin on Romeo and Juliet? (978-1-63679-444-0)

Wildflower by Cathleen Collins. When a plane crash leaves eleven-year-old Lily Andrews stranded in the vast wilderness of Arkansas, will she be able to overcome the odds and make it back to civilization and the one person who holds the key to her future? (978-1-63679-621-5)

Witch Finder by Sheri Lewis Wohl. Tasmin, the Keeper of the Book of Darkness, is in terrible danger, and as a Witch Finder, Morrigan must protect her and the secrets she guards even if it costs Morrigan her life. (978-1-63679-335-1)

Digging for Heaven by Jenna Jarvis. Litz lives for dragons. Kella lives to kill them. The last thing they expect is to find each other attractive. (978-1-63679-453-2)

Forever's Promise by Missouri Vaun. Wesley Holden migrated west disguised as a man for the hope of a better life and with no designs to take a wife, but Charlotte Rose has other ideas. (978-1-63679-221-7)

Here For You by D. Jackson Leigh. A horse trainer must make a difficult business decision that could save her father's ranch from foreclosure but destroy her chance to win the heart of a feisty barrel racer vying for a spot in the National Rodeo Finals. (978-1-63679-299-6)

I Do, I Don't by Joy Argento. Creator of the romance algorithm, Nicole Hart doesn't expect to be starring in her own reality TV dating show, and falling for the show's executive producer Annie Jackson could ruin everything. (978-1-63679-420-4)

It's All in the Details by Dena Blake. Makeup artist Lane Donnelly and wedding planner Helen Trent can't stand each other, but they must set aside their differences to ensure Darcy gets the wedding of her dreams, and make a few of their own dreams come true. (978-1-63679-430-3)

Marigold by Melissa Brayden. Marigold Lavender vows to take down Alexis Wakefield, the harsh food critic who blasts her younger sister's restaurant. If only she wasn't as sexy as she is mean. (978-1-63679-436-5)

A Second Chance at Life by Genevieve McCluer. Vampires Dinah and Rachel reconnect, but a string of vampire killings begin and evidence seems to be pointing at Dinah. They must prove her innocence while finding out if the two of them are still compatible after all these years. (978-1-63679-459-4)